D0426747

Hastings Memorial Library
505 Central Avenue
Grant, NE 69140

WITHDRAWN

1 THE WAY OF THE JEDI

Written by Jake T. Forbes

Grosset & Dunlap · LucasBooks

GROSSET & DUNLAP

Published by the Penguin Group

Penguin Group (USA) Inc., 375 Hudson Street, New York, New York 10014, USA

Penguin Group (Canada), 90 Eglinton Avenue East, Suite 700, Toronto, Ontario M4P 2Y3,

Canada (a division of Pearson Penguin Canada Inc.)

Penguin Books Ltd., 80 Strand, London WC2R 0RL, England

Penguin Group Ireland, 25 St. Stephen's Green, Dublin 2, Ireland

(a division of Penguin Books Ltd.)

Penguin Group (Australia), 250 Camberwell Road, Camberwell, Victoria 3124, Australia

(a division of Pearson Australia Group Pty. Ltd.)

Penguin Books India Pvt. Ltd., 11 Community Centre, Panchsheel Park,

New Delhi—110 017, India

Penguin Group (NZ), 67 Apollo Drive, Rosedale, North Shore 0632,

New Zealand (a division of Pearson New Zealand Ltd.)

Penguin Books (South Africa) (Pty.) Ltd., 24 Sturdee Avenue,

Rosebank, Johannesburg 2196, South Africa

Penguin Books Ltd., Registered Offices:

80 Strand, London WC2R 0RL, England

This book is published in partnership with LucasBooks, a division of Lucasfilm Ltd.
The scanning, uploading, and distribution of this book via the Internet or via any other means
without the permission of the publisher is illegal and punishable by law. Please purchase only
authorized electronic editions and do not participate in or encourage electronic piracy of
copyrighted materials. Your support of the author's rights is appreciated.
If you purchased this book without a cover, you should be aware that this book is stolen property.
It was reported as "unsold and destroyed" to the publisher, and neither the author nor the
publisher has received any payment for this "stripped book."
The publisher does not have any control over and does not assume any responsibility for author
or third-party websites or their content.
Copyright © 2008 Lucasfilm Ltd. & ® or ™ where indicated. All Rights Reserved. Used Under
Authorization. Published by Grosset & Dunlap, a division of Penguin Young Readers Group, 345
Hudson Street, New York, New York 10014. GROSSET & DUNLAP is a trademark of Penguin
Group (USA) Inc. Printed in the U.S.A.

Library of Congress Cataloging-in-Publication Data is available.

ISBN 978-0-448-45002-5   10 9 8 7 6 5 4

"Have you heard? Ahsoka was made Padawan!"

Of course you'd heard the news: *Everyone* has. It is all that your fellow initiates have been talking about since morning meditation. Even here in the Jedi Library, you find it hard to maintain a whisper.

Ahsoka Tano, top of her class in lightsaber skills and starship piloting alike, is already on her way to Christophsis to meet her new Master. And not just *any* Master, but Anakin Skywalker, barely shed of his Padawan braid and already a legend on the battlefield. It was a fitting match. The Togruta girl was one of the youngest initiates to ever be made Padawan, second only to Anakin himself. You're quite proud of your friend Ahsoka—a little jealous, perhaps, but proud. It seems your best friend Jaylen is taking things a little more personally . . .

"It's not fair!" Jaylen yells, drawing scolding glares from a nearby SP-4 model librarian droid. "I'm three years older than she is, and I'm a way better pilot."

Like you, Jaylen Kos has lived in the Jedi Temple for almost all of his life. The two of you have been best friends since your fifth year, when Master Drallig paired you up as sparring partners in his lightsaber class.

"Relax, Jaylen," you laugh. "When you get angry,

your face gets all red and you look like Darth Maul!"
And it's true . . . the young Zabrak does turn as red as
a Mandalorian beet when he loses his temper. "Besides,
Master Yoda wouldn't have assigned her if she wasn't
ready."

"Oh, yeah? Well, you're just defending her because
you have a crush on her," Jaylen replies with a huff.

Uh-oh . . . Your argument appears to have drawn the
attention of the library's robotic curator.

"Young Masters, need I remind you that while in the
library, voices must be kept below thirty decibels at all
times," the SP-4 drones. "Furthermore, any accusations
of amorous affection are to be reported to . . ." They can
program a droid to understand etiquette and protocol
from a thousand worlds, but they still can't make them
understand when you're just joking around!

You're about to apologize to the droid when you feel
a familiar hand pat you on the shoulder. "Thank you,
Espee. I'll speak with the younglings."

It's Jocasta Nu, Chief Librarian and a legend in the
Jedi Temple. "I know it can be difficult waiting to be
chosen by a Master when you are so close to Padawan
age," she tells you, "but you must trust in the wisdom of
Master Yoda and the Council."

Jaylen's temper is still getting the better of him. "But
how is anyone supposed to know we're ready when

all the Jedi are away at war? We want to help fight the Separatists, too! We're ready!"

Jocasta gives a gentle smile that calms you and Jaylen both. "How eager the young are to rush headlong into danger . . . The Force has a way of bringing Padawan and Master together, even when they are separated by star systems. When the time comes, you will find your Masters." Jocasta is about to return to her duties maintaining the Jedi Archives when she turns to you and Jaylen again. "Oh, I almost forgot! I believe Master Yoda wants to speak to both of you in the garden."

You and Jaylen look at each other in disbelief. "Master Yoda?" you exclaim. The Jedi Master and leaders of the Council don't often speak to initiates. Could this mean . . . ?!

Turn to page 80.

Master Eerin told you to stay by the ships, so that's just what you'll do. "We wait," you say to Jaylen.

It's not fear that keeps you from intervening, you tell yourself. Waiting is the right thing to do.

After what seems like hours, Ventress emerges from the facility, but she is not alone. Worker droids carry a large crate into the hold of the Confederate ship: That must be Bitt Panith's secret weapon. But there's something else being loaded. You tremble as you watch a troop of elite MagnaGuards, special droids trained to fight Jedi, drag a large brown sack out of the facility. On closer inspection, you see that it isn't a sack at all. It's an unconscious humanoid. Master Eerin!

"We should do something!" Jaylen shouts.

What could you possibly do to help, you think to yourself. You're too young . . . too weak . . .

"Are you okay?" Jaylen asks. When you don't respond he grips your shoulders and shakes. "Talk to me!" But it's too late. You let fear into your heart, and now fear has won.

THE END

The Republic gunship touches down in a small clearing two miles from Quaagan's base. Maintaining your plan, the clone troopers equip their grappling hooks and set out on foot for the base of the cliff.

Chewbacca is as able a guide as you could have asked for. The Wookiee leads your men through Kashyyyk's strange and deadly forests, pointing out invisible patches of quicksand just off the trail and flesh-eating gorryl slugs hiding in the branches.

At last you emerge, undetected, at the base of the cliff. Far up on the cliff face you see a Confederate ship parked on a rock outcropping. Grakchawwaa was right; Quaagan *is* dealing with the Separatists!

"You've been a great guide, Chewbacca, but we can take things from here," you tell your Wookiee companion. "We'll meet you here on the way back, all right, friend?"

Chewbacca moans in agreement.

You join the clone troopers as they fire their ropes up the cliff face and begin the ascent. Like silent ghosts, you and your team walk up the vertical cliff face until you are just below the ledge where Quaagan and his traitorous associates are.

As you pull yourself up onto the ledge, you quickly

scan the environment for any signs of the enemy. Nothing could have prepared you for what you find. Quaagan, the white-haired Wookiee traitor, is speaking to none other than Asajj Ventress, Count Dooku's personal assassin. Even more shocking is who is standing next to Ventress. It is your friend, Jaylen Kos!

Turn to page 43.

When you come to, you and Jaylen and Sunchoo are lying in the center of a large arena. The stands all around you are filled with Separatist alien races, cheering in anticipation of your demise.

A voice booms from the arena speakers, "Friends of the Confederacy! It is with great pleasure that we present to you the execution of these foul Jedi and their mangy companion!" The crowd erupts in applause.

"Do you think the Jedi Council will find us here?" Jaylen asks.

"I don't even know where here is," you reply.

Suddenly the crowds grow silent as a large metal grate on the side of the arena opens. From out of the darkness walks not one, but *two* mighty rancors. After Anakin Skywalker's and Obi-Wan Kenobi's escape from the arena of Geonosis, it appears as if this time the Separatists aren't taking any chances.

Sunchoo whimpers with fear.

"Don't worry, Sunchoo. When Master Eerin notices that we've gone missing, I'm sure she'll come to rescue us," you say. But as much as you want to believe that, you know it's unlikely help will arrive in time.

THE END

"Clearly has the Force spoken to me. Chosen the Padawan, I have," Yoda announces. "Step forward, Jaylen Kos."

So it isn't your day after all. First Ahsoka, now Jaylen. Pretty soon you'll be the last member of your clan not fighting in the Clone Wars. But wait! Yoda isn't finished speaking . . .

"Jaylen Kos, a brave Jedi I see you becoming . . . but not today," Yoda says, his green brow furrowed. "Quick to anger, you are. And even quicker to leap with eyes closed, headlong into danger. Temperance you must learn before into battle I will send you."

Jaylen's response is immediate. His face turns redder than you've ever seen it before. "But . . . but, Master Yoda! I'm ready! I swear it! I'll prove it to you!" Before you can say anything, Jaylen runs from the garden. Yoda shakes his head like a disappointed parent. But if Jaylen's not the new Padawan, then that means . . .

Yoda raises his wrinkled hand and points it at you. "Bant Eerin's Padawan *you* shall be."

"Master Yoda," you say. "When can I meet Master Eerin?"

"Already departed for her mission, Eerin has.

Follow her. Debrief you, she will. Depart at once, you must, for the Kashyyyk system."

So this is it. You're a Padawan now. "Thank you, Master Yoda. I will not let you down."

Yoda looks at you sternly, as if to hold you to those words. "Hmm . . . We will see. May the Force be with you."

Turn to page 50.

You think back on your Jedi training and remember something Master Windu once said: "A wise Jedi knows when victory can be won alone, and when it requires the might of an army." This is clearly a case of the latter. If only you can find a way to contact the Council back on Coruscant . . .

That's it! You can hack into the facility's communications systems to send a low-frequency transmission back to your ship, then have R3-G0 relay it to the Republic. You rip the casing off the first comm panel you find and manually adjust the wiring, all the while hoping that your "friend" the janitor hasn't recovered enough from his mental manipulation to call for help. Thirty seconds later, you hear the comforting beeps of your astromech droid. "Argo, I need you to send this transmission on all Republic frequencies." He chirps back in the affirmative.

"Allies of the Republic," you say into the transmitter. "I am a member of the Jedi Order, held prisoner by Separatist forces on the Trandoshan moon of Akoshissss. If you can hear this message, please send . . ."

Suddenly the sparking purple blade of an electrostaff slashes through the console, cutting your transmission short. You've been discovered! Your MagnaGuard captors grip your shoulders and spin you around so that you're face-to-face with Bitt Panith.

"You Jedi certainly have a knack for making things difficult," the fiend says.

"What should we do with the prisoners?" one of the MagnaGuards asks.

Doctor Panith scratches his chin as he considers his options. "Now that our location is compromised, we have to leave, of that there is no question," he says. "As for the prisoners . . . leave them. Perhaps this act of mercy will spare us the Jedi's wrath."

The droids drag you back to your holding cell. Soon you are rejoined by Jaylen. He doesn't appear injured.

By the time the Jedi Council sends a rescue party, Bitt Panith and everyone involved with his research are gone, and the computer databanks are wiped. You never did find out what his top secret project was. While you will live to see another day, you can't help but wonder what trouble Doctor Panith will cause for the Jedi in the future. Perhaps you'll be there to fight him again. Only time will tell.

THE END

"I've always received top marks in military tactics," you say. "With your permission, Master, I think I could best serve the mission by leading the troops on the ground."

Master Eerin nods. "Very well. Captain Herc, you and your men will report to my Padawan for the duration of the operation. I will take care of the other teams."

Now it's just you and the clone soldiers under your command. While these genetically identical men appear to be twice your age, you know that they're actually younger and that growth acceleration is what made them so large and imposing. Even so, these clones have known nothing but battle since the day they emerged from their cloning chambers. It won't be easy to earn their respect, as one clone with red swatches on his armor makes clear. "Pardon me, sir, but why should we take orders from a youngling?"

"Sergeant Troy! You will show our Padawan commander the proper respect, or you'll be heading the charge without a blaster." That seems to have put Sergeant Troy in his place . . . for now.

Captain Herc calls your attention to the holoprojector map. "Commander, as you can see, in order to reach the shield generator, we will need to get through the droid defenses here and here," he says, pointing out the units on the 3-D display.

"I understand," you say. "I will remain on foot with the infantry, providing backup for the AT-TEs. Once the shields are down, you bring in the gunships to take out the remaining droid defenders."

Down to the battlefield you go! Mighty AT-TE tanks and their smaller cousins, the AT-PT scout walkers, roar to life around you. Several miles ahead you can see the shield generator and the droid units defending it. You walk to the front of the infantry, igniting your lightsaber and waving it like a flag to signal the start of the assault. Onward!

Turn to page 129.

You arrive in the Kashyyyk system, home to the noble Wookiees and savage reptilian Trandoshans. This is farther from the Galactic Core than you've ever been before. And you're all alone . . . or are you? Something doesn't feel right. You feel another presence nearby. You slowly turn around to check the rear of the cockpit, when all of a sudden . . .

"AAAAGH!" you scream upon seeing a pair of eyes staring at you from the darkness.

"Calm down, silly," a familiar voice says. "It's me!"

"Jaylen!" No wonder you couldn't find him in the dormitory. He was busy stowing away on your ship!

"You didn't think I'd let you have an adventure without me, did you?" he asks with a mischievous smile. "How else am I going to prove myself to the Council?"

"This is serious," you say. Before you can finish your thought, you are interrupted by an incoming transmission on a private channel. "Padawan, is that you?"

Turn to page 32.

Goomi leads you down into the dark undergrowth of Kashyyyk where even Wookiees fear to tread. "Are you sure this is the right way?" you ask your guide.

"Oh, yes. Crovan comes down here to hunt. We're almost there," Goomi replies enthusiastically. "There! His camp is just ahead."

Crovan Dane is not alone. His partner is a ragged Wookiee mercenary with a patch on one eye. "That is Tahnchukka, Crovan's partner," Goomi explains. "Strong as gundark. Very dangerous."

As you approach the edge of the camp, Goomi motions for you and Jaylen to hide. "Stay here until I call for you," he says. "Crovan's in for quite a surprise!"

Goomi steps into the clearing, a blaster in his hands and a smile on his snout. "Well, if it isn't Crovan Dane. Thought you could leave the planet without paying your debt, did you?"

Crovan raises his hands and speaks calmly. "No one's running, Goomi. You can tell your boss we'll have his credits as soon as we deliver this shipment to Bitt Panith on Akoshissss."

"You have made Master Ziro wait long enough, smuggler," Goomi says. "And the Hutts do *not* like to be kept waiting."

Ziro the Hutt? He's only one of the vilest gangsters on Coruscant! So *that's* who Goomi works for.

"Strong words, Goomi. But there are two of us and one of you," Crovan says, nodding toward Tahnchukka.

Goomi laughs. "You do not think I am foolish enough to come without backup of my own? I have Jedi on my side!"

That's your signal. If you're going to help Goomi in this standoff, now is the time to act. On the other hand, Goomi is a criminal himself. Maybe it would be best to stay out of this conflict . . .

If you assist Goomi with his hostile takeover, turn to page 160.

If you stay hidden, turn to page 117.

You wake up on the stone floor of makeshift arena. The pit is empty except for a large metal door. You can guess who will be coming through it. Up above you can see Doctor Panith and his assistants watching you and taking notes on their datapads. To your right is Jaylen, still unconscious.

"Jaylen," you shout. "Wake up!"

"Ngh . . ." Jaylen wakes up with a groan. "Where are we?"

"We're in a heap of trouble, that's where," you quip. And you couldn't be more correct. The huge door is creaking open and behind it you can hear the metallic clanks of Krossen's footsteps. If only you had your lightsaber . . . No, the lightsaber would do you no good against this Force-resistant monstrosity. A tingling sensation surges through your body as the heightened senses you came to rely on from your training fade away. You wish you were back at the Jedi Temple where failure meant a slap on the wrist, not certain doom.

"Well, Jaylen," you say. "Are you still glad you stowed away on my ship?"

THE END

"Focus AT-TE fire on the hailfire droids," you order the clones. "They're our most immediate concern."

The lumbering tanks strain to get a lock, but the hailfire droids are too nimble. *Boom!* Another AT-TE has gone down in flames. With just one AT-TE left, your clone soldiers manage to take out one of the hailfires. Now all hope rests on the one remaining AT-TE. *Kaboom!* That hope dies in a fiery explosion.

"Good call on those hailfires, Commander," Sergeant Troy mocks over the radio. "Did they teach you that strategy at the Jedi Academy?"

Blast it! If those shields stay up, Master Eerin won't be able to lead her team into the Separatist base. With the AT-TEs gone, it is up to *you* to bring down the shield by yourself!

Turn to page 95.

"The cargo you carry is part of a plot to defeat the Jedi," you explain to Crovan and Tahnchukka. "I can't allow it to fall into the hands of the Separatists."

Crovan Dane scoffs. "Then you might as well kill me now, Jedi, because if I don't get the credits to pay off Ziro, I'm a dead man. Every bounty hunter in the sector will be after me."

"Perhaps the Jedi Order can help," you suggest. "Release the beasts you were planning to take to Panith and my friend and I will plead your case to the Jedi Council."

Crovan confers with his Wookiee friend, and then turns to you. "We don't have much of a choice, do we?"

The pair of smugglers release cage after cage of savage beasts from the back of their ship. You shudder to think of what a mad cyberneticist like Panith would do with such creatures.

Now that the cargo is taken care of, you head back to Coruscant with Crovan Dane in tow.

Turn to page 127.

The young Wookiee bows to you and speaks with affectionate growls. "My name is Sunchoo. You have saved me from a life of slavery in the service of that vile man, and for that, I am forever in your debt."

"It was nothing," you assure her. "All in the line of duty as a Jedi."

Sunchoo shakes her shaggy head. "You do not understand, great Jedi. A Life Debt is a most serious matter. I cannot leave until the debt is repaid. I may be young, but I am as brave as the great hunters and I know every tree in this forest."

You take a closer look at your new friend. Much of her silky hair is tied into braids with wildflowers woven in. She does look almost like a child. "Just how old are you?" you ask. "We could use your help, but our mission is dangerous; it is not a task for a child."

Sunchoo averts her eyes, and beneath her hairy face, you can almost see her blushing. "I am only forty-three years old, but the elders say I am very mature for my age." Forty-three? She's old enough to be your mother!

You're still not sure about this "Life Debt," but it's nice to have a guide who knows Kashyyyk as well as Sunchoo does. After you and Jaylen introduce yourselves, you tell her about your mission and the dead end you've hit in your search for Crovan Dane.

At the mention of your target's name, Sunchoo perks up. "Crovan Dane? He calls himself a bounty hunter, but he is really nothing more than a slaver. That black-hearted cur is the one who stole me from my village! I will take you to him. Come, we must hurry!"

It appears that your luck is finally turning around.

Turn to page 83.

"We're checking out the signal," you say. "That's final."

You leave the research facility behind and track the distress beacon to its source on the far side of Akoshissss. The signal appears to be emanating from a disabled cargo freighter. What's more troubling are the half-dozen disabled starfighters and salvage ships that float around the freighter. Among the debris is a familiar red and white Delta-7B *Aethersprite*.

"A Jedi starfighter!" Jaylen exclaims.

You have R3-G0 scan the ships. "That's Master Eerin's ship all right, but there's no pilot. I am picking up faint life signs from the freighter . . . I can't tell if it's her. We're going to have to dock with the ship to find out."

"This definitely stinks of a trap," Jaylen says. "If we're not careful, we'll end up dead in the water just like Master Eerin."

"Then we'll just have to be careful," you say.

Turn to page 155.

"We'll never surrender to you!" you yell as you and Jaylen ignite your lightsabers.

Lightsaber combat was your strongest suit back at the Jedi Temple, and you put your skills to good use against the chameleon droids. The glowing green blade of your lightsaber cuts through droid after droid, leaving piles of scrap in your wake. Ahead of you Jaylen deflects an incoming laser shot into another droid, frying its circuits. For one glorious moment, you believe you can destroy them all!

But in the end, a human and a Zabrak can't fight forever, whereas the droid army never tires. More and more chameleon droids materialize from the wasteland. For every droid you slice in half, two more appear. You start to sweat. Your legs feel like jelly. You can't last much longer. "Jaylen!" you cry to your friend, perhaps for help, perhaps for a final good-bye, but you get no response. After hundreds of perfect swings, you make your first mistake, but that's all it takes. A laser blast hits you in your saber hand, making you drop your blade. Now you're completely defenseless. If the droid's lasers don't kill you, their razor-sharp pincer legs will.

THE END

"Nice throw, rookie," Sergeant Troy says. "But it seems our efforts came too late."

As you survey the war-torn fields of Akoshissss, you see that he's right. During the delay in taking down the shields, the droid army got the upper hand on the battlefield. The Republic gunships that were supposed to turn the tide in your favor lie smoldering in ruins. Your remaining clone troopers are clustered in a circle as they make a last stand against the encroaching droid forces. You can see Bant Eerin and Jaylen in the crowd, their lightsabers flaring. You wonder if Master Eerin succeeded in her mission.

"As long as any Republic soldier is standing, we can't give up the fight," you say. "Let's join the others." Troy nods in agreement.

The clone troopers are glad to have you and Sergeant Troy fighting by their sides, but your arrival does little to change the odds. It's a losing battle. More and more clones fall to droid blasters.

Turn to page 111.

Your adrenaline is still pumping from your victory over that bounty hunter. You feel like you can take on the galaxy yourselves. "Let's do it!" you say.

Jaylen heads to the surface of Akoshissss and sets the ship down as close as he can without getting in sensor range of the secret facility.

Once you are on the moon's surface, you pull out your electrobinoculars and scan the horizon to see what kind of security measures Bitt Panith has in place. As far as you can tell, it's a clear path from here to the research facility. "It looks safe," you say. "Almost *too* safe."

You notice Jaylen staring hard to the west of your landing site. "I think I see something over there," he says. "It looks like a cave. Maybe it's a secret entrance!"

If you would rather investigate the cave, turn to page 40.

If you decide to take the direct approach, turn to page 103.

You make your way back to the spaceport where you left Chewbacca and R3-G0, but when you arrive, you see someone you weren't expecting. Jedi Master Bant Eerin is there, in the flesh this time. She is accompanied by a Republic gunship crewed by a dozen clone troopers, all ready for battle.

"Master Eerin?" you say.

"Apprehending Bitt Panith took shorter than expected," Eerin explains. "And so I decided to accompany the clones in coming to your aid here on Kashyyyk. When I arrived, I was a bit upset to discover you had disappeared."

"A-about that, Master Eerin . . ." you stammer.

"Chewbacca here told me about what happened after you contacted me. I see you were able to persuade young Jaylen to reconsider his decision?"

Jaylen steps forward. "You are correct, Master Eerin. I almost made a great mistake. Your Padawan, *my friend*, showed me that."

Bant Eerin nods serenely. "You are not the first Jedi to question his place with the Jedi Order, Jaylen Kos. If you are willing to give the Council one more chance, I think they might surprise you with their understanding." Eerin turns her gaze to your two prisoners and adds, "I see that you found someone else on your adventure."

"Yes, Master Eerin," you say. "We found Crovan Dane. He was hunting beasts to sell to Bitt Panith."

"It seems the Force was with us both on this mission, my Padawan," Eerin says.

Chewbacca the Wookiee makes an inquiring moan.

"That's right," Master Eerin replies. "We still have the matter of King Grakchawwaa's traitor to deal with." She turns to you and asks, "What do you say, Padawan, should we handle this mission together?"

You can scarcely contain your excitement. Master and apprentice, fighting together to defend the galaxy. This is where your Jedi training really begins!

THE END

You motion to Jaylen and Lex to follow, then make your way up the ramp into Panith's cargo ship.

No sooner are you inside the door of the ship, you see a crimson smoke filling the hangar. It's some kind of poison gas! Up ahead R3-G0 docks with the ship's console and shuts the door behind you. Through the cockpit window, you can see the MagnaGuards, immune to the poison gas and furious that their trap failed to catch you. They have out their flickering electrostaffs. You had better act fast.

As quick as you can, you switch on the ship's repulsorlift engines to make it hover, then slam the control stick forward. "Everybody, hold on!"

Bam! The ship lurches forward, slamming into the MagnaGuards and squishing them flat against the wall of the hangar.

Once the gas in the hangar has cleared, you and your team exit the ship. "All right, Sergeant," you say. "Ready those explosives and let's get out of here."

Turn to page 77.

"All right, Jaylen," you say. "I don't agree with what you're doing, but as your friend, I will let you choose your own destiny." You put down your lightsaber and start to walk away from the clearing, perhaps never to see your friend again.

"Not so fast, Padawan," Crovan says. "I've still got work to finish up on Kashyyyk and I can't have you telling anyone of my whereabouts."

You look to Jaylen to see his response to the mercenary's threat. "I-it's all right, Crovan. Y-you can trust my friend not to tell."

Crovan shakes his head. "If you're coming with me, kid, there's a few things you've got to learn. First rule of being a mercenary: Never trust a Jedi."

With his blaster pointed right at your chest, Crovan pulls the trigger. There's no way you're escaping this time.

Will Jaylen avenge you? Or will he follow this killer and take up a lawless life? You'll never know now. If you really cared, perhaps you should have said something sooner.

THE END

"Master Eerin!" you reply. "Yoda sent me to help you with the mission. Where can I meet you?"

"I'm afraid we're going to have to postpone introductions," Eerin says. "Right now I'm in pursuit of Doctor Bitt Panith, a Muun cyberneticist who assisted with the creation of General Grievous's robotic body. I've tracked him to his base on the Trandoshan moon of Akoshissss and will strike as soon as my clone troopers arrive. While I coordinate the attack, I need you to head to Kashyyyk and find a bounty hunter named Crovan Dane who has been helping Panith. *Ksshhh*—very dangerous—*zzssh* . . ."

"Master, you're breaking up. What's going on?!"

"Well, Jaylen, looks like you're coming with me on this mission after all," you say. "But what do we do? Go to Kashyyyk and find this Crovan guy, or head for the Akoshissss to check on Master Eerin?"

"You're the Padawan," Jaylen says. "It's your call."

If you go to Akoshissss, turn to page 34.
If you go to Kashyyyk, turn to page 58.

You return to Coruscant in triumph. Several weeks later Master Bant Eerin summons you from your quarters. "We have a new assignment, Padawan, in the Ryloth system. Apparently General Grievous is stirring up trouble in the Outer Rim."

You can scarcely hide your enthusiasm. The Ryloth system is a dangerous place, but also very beautiful, or so you've heard from your Twi'lek friends. "Will it just be the two of us, Master Eerin?" you ask.

"As a matter of fact," Eerin says, "Master Yoda is sending another Jedi Knight and Padawan with us. Someone I think you'll be happy to see."

Suddenly a familiar voice calls out behind you. "Guess who, Padawan?" a familiar voice calls out.

"Jaylen!" you cry. "Don't tell me you're . . ."

"Coming with you to Ryloth," Jaylen interrupts.

This is fantastic! Another adventure awaits—the first of many, you are sure—and once again, you'll have your best friend by your side. Only this time you'll have the blessing of the Council.

THE END

"We're going to Akoshissss," you say. "Master Eerin's in trouble. Argo, see if you can get a fix on Master Eerin's last known coordinates."

R3-G0 gives an affirmative beep and feeds the data into the ship's computer. You head for Akoshissss, pushing your sublight engines to their limit. When you make it to the coordinates, however, there's no sign of Bant Eerin's starfighter or evidence of a fight.

"She must have escaped," you suggest. "She's probably down there already, infiltrating the base."

"I don't know," Jaylen says. "If that's the case, wouldn't she have tried to regain contact with you?"

He's got a point. Suddenly, you're interrupted by a panicked whoop from R3-G0. "Argo's picking up a distress signal from the other side of the moon."

"Master Eerin's ship?" Jaylen asks.

"Negative," you reply. "It's a civilian frequency."

"It could be a trap," Jaylen suggests.

If you investigate the signal, turn to page 114.

If you head down to the moon's surface instead, turn to page 142.

The forward command center is alive with activity. Clone mechanics ready the lumbering AT-TE walkers, while clone commandos strap on the latest in Republic weaponry for the assault. And overseeing it from a raised platform is a Mon Calamari woman clothed in the familiar robes of a Jedi Knight.

"Master Eerin!" you yell.

Bant Ecrin looks you up and down with a stern gaze. "Did you not hear me order you to Kashyyyk, Padawan?"

Oh no! You've only just met your new Master and already she seems disappointed. "I did, Master," you respond with as much confidence as you can muster. "But it sounded as if you were under attack. We couldn't . . ."

The stern look gives way to a gentle smile. "Do not apologize; you followed your heart. You made the right choice, Padawan. Welcome." Master Eerin's turns her gaze to Jaylen. "But who is this? He looks too young to be traveling without a Master."

Jaylen explains how he stowed away, breaking a dozen rules in the process. When he is done, he looks to the ground as if awaiting punishment.

"You will have to answer to the Council for this

when we return, but right now I need every able body for the upcoming battle," Master Eerin says. "For the duration of this mission, you will stay with me at the command center."

Jaylen gets to stay with your new Master? But what about you, the Padawan?

As if sensing your disappointment, Bant Eerin adds, "As for you, my Padawan, the time has come for you to get a taste of command."

Turn to page 53.

"Argo's on his own. I'm not going to let that crazy droid get us all captured," you say. "Sergeant Lex, set up those explosives. Jaylen and I will keep a look out for the MagnaGuards."

As the clone commando sets to his task, you take a moment to hone your senses. If you can't see the MagnaGuards, perhaps you can feel their presence with the Force. Suddenly your ears become attuned to a barely audible hiss. You scan the room until your eye stops at a spot in the corner. Something's definitely wrong up there: There's a crimson gas flowing out of the air vents!

"Jaylen, Lex, we've got to get out of here!" you call out to your team.

Quickly, you run back the way you came. Ahead you can see the blast door sealing off your exit. A few more seconds and you'll be trapped. At the last moment you and Jaylen dive through the doorway and roll to safety. Sergeant Lex, with his heavy armor, can't make it in time.

Lex's voice crackles through the communicator in your ear. "The mission isn't over yet, Commander. I can still set the explosives." Through the window in the hangar doors you see Sergeant Lex setting to his task, but the poison gas is starting to affect him. "It's going to be . . . a big bang, sir . . . I suggest . . . you . . . run . . ."

"Lex? Lex?!" But it's no use. The clone commando has passed out from the gas. "This is all my fault," you mutter to yourself. "I should have listened to Argo . . ."

You are snapped back to reality by Jaylen tugging on your robe. "There's no time for that. You heard the sergeant. We've got to move!"

Turn to page 42.

"All right, Sunchoo. We'll stay back for now," you say. "But we're not going to abandon you. If anything goes wrong, call out and we'll be there in a flash."

Sunchoo nods, then turns herself in to Tahnchukka and his boss.

"Well, what have we here? Didn't I already sell you to the Neimoidian, girl?" Crovan asks. "No matter. We'll just sell you to someone else and collect another payment. Come on, Tank. Let's put her back with the others."

The gray Wookiee points his bowcaster at Sunchoo's back and leads her up into Crovan's ship. Before she disappears into the hold, Sunchoo looks back toward your hiding spot and winks.

"Follow me, Jaylen," you say, sneaking closer to Crovan's ship and the stacks of cages. "I've got a plan."

Turn to page 92.

"All right, let's check out this cave," you agree. "Argo, you stay here and watch the ship." R3-G0 gives an affirmative beep as you and Jaylen march across the crunchy regolith waste toward the cave entrance.

The cave is perfectly round and about thirty feet in diameter. There doesn't appear to be any security here . . .

"What are you waiting for?" Jaylen nags. "Let's go!"

Down, down, down you go into the mysterious cave. All you hear is the sound of your footsteps on gravel. *Crunch. Crunch. Crunch. Squish. Squish?* "I've got a bad feeling about this . . ." you say.

"Can't you feel it? The air is getting warmer!" Jaylen says. "I think we're almost to the end."

Suddenly the ground starts shaking beneath you. "What's going on?" Jaylen asks. "Is this an earthquake?"

You pull out your flashlight and scan the cave walls. They're slick and dripping with mucus. "This is no cave," you say. "Run!" You spin around and head back the way you came as fast as your legs will carry you. Up ahead you can see what appears to be a cave-in as jagged white stones clamp down to seal off the entrance. But you know those aren't stones . . . they're teeth. You've wandered right into the belly of an exorgoth space slug!

There are only a few more yards to go. You can still make it to the surface before the slug traps you in its maw! To your right you see Jaylen sprinting past you. He dives through the entrance just as the enormous exorgoth teeth clamp shut.

"Jaylen!" you shout. "Jaylen, make it open!" But no amount of screaming and pounding will save you now. From the back of the tunnel you can hear the gurgling of a million gallons of digestive fluids surging toward you. It could be worse, you think. At least it's not a Sarlacc.

THE END

Whether it's luck or the Force that's guiding you, somehow you and Jaylen find your way back out of Doctor Panith's mazelike compound. Moments after you emerge, you hear and feel an explosion so loud you're afraid it will crack the moon right open.

Master Bant Eerin is waiting for you at the forward command post. "There were four when you left, now there are but two. Tell me what happened, Padawan."

You explain about the trap, and about Argo and Sergeant Lex. "I'm sorry, Master," you say. "I have let you down."

"No, my Padawan. A Jedi cannot measure everything in black or white. Today was not a defeat," Eerin says. "It was a compromised victory. We should count our successes, and mourn our losses."

That night the clone troopers hold a wake for those who were lost in battle. As you watch from a distance, you are amazed that these soldiers, so identical in appearance, can feel so deeply. The next time it is your responsibility, and honor, to lead these men in battle, you will do everything in your power to see that every last one of them comes home alive.

THE END

"Jaylen!" you call out in disbelief. "What are you doing here? With *her*?!"

Asajj Ventress places a hand on Jaylen's shoulder. He lowers his eyes, afraid to meet your gaze. "I always suspected our teachers at the Jedi Temple were just holding me back," Jaylen says. "Asajj Ventress has shown me the true power of the Force."

You feel betrayal welling up inside you as your best friend challenges everything you've ever believed in.

"You don't know what you're saying, Jaylen! Help defeat these traitors," you plead.

"The only traitor here is you," Jaylen says. "You betrayed me when you chose the mission over me."

"That's not true," you say. "You are letting anger cloud your judgment."

Jaylen shakes his head. "No, old friend. I see clearer than I've ever seen before. Let's settle this here and now. No rules, just the two of us and our lightsabers. What do you say?"

If you accept Jaylen's challenge, turn to page 93.
If you decline Jaylen's challenge, turn to page 97.

You still can't believe it. Jaylen is dead . . . by your hand. The clone troopers look to you for guidance, but you have none to give them.

Asajj Ventress approaches you and says, "From the moment Jaylen Kos came here, I knew that he was weak. He was not in touch with his emotions, not the way that you are."

You back away from the assassin. "That's not true. It can't be true. I am a Jedi!"

The assassin smiles and shakes her head. "No, young one. You will never be a Jedi now. Not after what you did."

She's right. Master Eerin will disown you for sure. Master Yoda will ban you from the Jedi Order. Maybe you'll even be sent to prison!

When Ventress looks into your eyes, you see actual compassion. At least, that's what you want to see. "But what you did was not wrong. You were strong. Come with me and I will help you become stronger still. I will show you the ways of the dark side."

Ventress holds her pale hand toward you. You close your eyes and take it.

THE END

"Bona nai kachu, Goomi. Dunchoka mawa bunko Jedi otanga!" Ziro replies in Huttese.

"But, Master Ziro! Had I known that the Jedi were watching you, I would never have—"

"Kava doompa stoopa, Goomi. Tacoocha poodoo!" Ziro makes a slitting motion with his slimy arm.

The MagnaGuards grab Goomi by the arms and lead the panicking shapeshifter out of the office.

With Goomi gone, the Hutt gangster summons a protocol droid to help translate for you. "The great and powerful Ziro the Hutt apologizes for any inconvenience Goomi caused you," the droid says. "You will of course be released at once. As for the shipment taken from Crovan, Master Ziro will keep that for his inconvenience."

"You are free to go, Jedi. But do not return to this place again or Master Ziro will not be so forgiving."

Crovan Dane was stopped, but you doubt this was the course of actions your Master, Bant Eerin, would have taken. You turn to Jaylen, still confused by the odd turn of events. "That was weird."

"Tell me about it," Jaylen agrees.

THE END

You return to the spaceport to find R3-G0 waiting patiently by your starship. "See if you can contact Master Eerin on Akoshissss," you tell the astromech droid. R3-G0 beeps in acknowledgement and a few moments later your Jedi Master appears before you as a shimmering blue hologram.

"Master Eerin! Thank goodness you're safe," you say. "After your transmission cut out, I was worried that you were under attack."

"It was nothing too dangerous, my Padawan. Just a few vulture droids that I reduced to scrap metal," Bant Eerin responds. "How goes your search for Crovan Dane?"

You tell Master Eerin about your friend and about your audience with Grakchawwaa and your promise to assist the Wookiee king in dealing with the traitor Quaagan.

"You were dealt a difficult choice, my Padawan. Time will tell if you made the right one. But now we must honor the promise you made the Wookiees," Eerin says. "I cannot join you yet. I must finish things here on Akoshissss, but I can send a division of clone troopers to assist you."

"Thank you, Master Eerin," you say. "I promise

not to let you down."

"Very well, Padawan. Now, before I take my leave, is there anything else you wish to tell me?"

There is something Master Eerin doesn't know about . . . *someone*. To your side, Jaylen is shaking his head with a panicked look on his face.

Turn to page 158.

You and Jaylen sneak into the laboratory first, leaving Lex and Argo to watch for the MagnaGuards.

In the center of the room is an enormous cyborg strapped to an operating table, apparently lifeless. Doctor Panith is kneeling before a holoprojector. "The Jedi are here on Akoshissss, your vileness," the scientist says. "I will transfer my data and the prototype to my shuttle, but it will be some time before Project Krossen will be ready for mass production."

Projected before the Muun scientist is the glowing blue hologram of a face every Jedi knows and fears: Count Dooku! "You disappoint me, Doctor Panith," the Sith Lord says. "Perhaps I should have the Banking Guild withdraw your funding."

"If you do, my Lord, you would be entirely justified, of course," Panith says. "But I assure you, when my cyborg soldiers are complete, the Jedi will crumble before us."

"See that they do, Doctor." And with that, Dooku's projected image flickers then cuts out.

Bitt Panith is still trembling from his exchange with the supreme leader of the Separatist forces. "Threaten to cut my funding, will you? After all that I've done for the Confederacy?"

You and Jaylen step out from behind your hiding spot, your lightsabers drawn. "Right now you've got bigger things to worry about than your funding, Panith," you say. "You're under arrest."

"Jedi!" Panith cries. "My masterpiece isn't complete, but he should still be strong enough for the likes of you!" The mad Muun scientist backs away from you and presses a button sequence on his computer terminal. Suddenly lights flicker across the cyborg body strapped to the table and the metal binding straps snap off. Krossen is activated!

Turn to page 106.

This is it! Your first mission. And your new Master, Bant Eerin, should make an excellent teacher. After all, she was Padawan to Kit Fisto, a member of the Jedi High Council and one of the greatest generals in the Clone Wars. You've also heard that Master Eerin is a close friend of Obi-Wan Kenobi. Perhaps in your journeys you'll cross paths with Ahsoka before too long.

You hurry to the hangar where your trusty astromech droid R3-G0 is already readying your new starfighter for the journey to the Kashyyyk system. Well, maybe "trusty" isn't the best word to describe "Argo." You probably logged as many hours repairing your droid as you did in pilot training. Jaylen used to joke that if things didn't work out for you as a Jedi, you could always fall back on a career in cybernetics.

Oh! That reminds you, you never got a chance to say good-bye to Jaylen. He wasn't in the dormitory when you grabbed your equipment. Where could he have gone? Oh well, it will have to wait until you get back. Right now, the mission comes first.

"All right, Argo," you say to the droid as you climb into the cockpit of your Delta-7B class starfighter. "Take us to Kashyyyk."

"*Brp bip boeep!*" R3-G0 confirms with an upbeat stream of binary beeps, and spins in a little 180-degree circle on the hangar floor before docking with the ship.

You feel the ship start to sway as the repulsorlift kicks in. "I'll take it from here," you tell R3-G0. "I need to get a feel for this new ship." You pilot the nimble starfighter out of the hangar and take it into orbit. Behind you, you see the enormous spires of the Jedi Temple recede into the distance until they are lost completely in the glittering sprawl of Coruscant. Once you're outside of the planet's atmosphere, you dock your ship with a hyperspace transport ring. Now you're ready for the jump to lightspeed.

"Next stop, the Kashyyyk system!"

Turn to page 16.

Krossen lunges toward you with its enormous arm. You dive to the side, barely escaping its grasp. Jaylen isn't so lucky. The cyborg monster has your friend by the throat and lifts him up into the air.

Suddenly Sergeant Lex bursts through the doors behind you. "Force immunity, huh? Let's see how immune it is to a good old-fashioned blaster," the clone commando says. He fires a perfect shot right into Krossen's chest, knocking him back.

While you are focused on Krossen, Doctor Panith sneaks out through the laboratory's back door. "Have fun with the prototype, Jedi fools. I can always make more."

"The three of us can hold off this monster," Lex says. "You go get that madman before he escapes. Finish the mission, Commander."

You can stay and help them or you can try and stop Panith, but you can't do both.

If you stay and battle Krossen, turn to page 99.
If you take off after Panith, turn to page 57.

Here on the battlefield, your Master is a general. And as her apprentice, you, too, are an officer. You look out over the rows of clone soldiers. Each of these men is counting on you for guidance and suddenly the seriousness of your position sinks in. "What would you have me do, Master?" you ask.

"Our objective remains the same as when you first left Coruscant: We must apprehend the rogue scientist Bitt Panith. Only the scale of the operation has changed." Bant Eerin presses a few keys on her console to bring up a holoprojected map of Akoshissss.

"This battle will be fought on three fronts," she continues. "First, a ground assault force will need to take down the shield generator, here.

"A second smaller team will infiltrate Bitt Panith's base from a secret entrance over here. This team will attempt to arrest Panith, or, failing that, destroy the laboratory and his research.

"Finally, a single diplomatic representative must travel to Trandosha. The Trandoshans are not allied with the Separatists, at least not openly, but they have no love for the Republic. They might see this battle as an attempt to usurp their authority in the region, which could tip them firmly into the Separatist camp. This must not be allowed to happen."

Master Eerin turns to you and says, "Padawan, *you* must lead one of these three teams."

If you choose to lead the clone troopers into battle, turn to page 14.

If you would rather lead a small strike squad into the compound, turn to page 68.

If you head to Trandosha to try and smooth over relations with the Trandoshans, turn to page 115.

Back on Coruscant, Jaylen Kos is summoned to the Jedi Council to answer for his disobedience. You wait in the dormitory for his return for what seems like hours. At last he shows up, but his manner isn't what you expected. He's positively beaming with excitement. "Did you get off with a light punishment?" you ask.

"Not at all," Jaylen replies. "They've got me doing extra lessons for the next month."

"Then what are you so happy about?"

Jaylen smiles. "It turns out my little stunt attracted a lot of attention. A Jedi Master saw something in me and wants me as his Padawan! Master Yoda says that as long as I stay out of trouble, I can begin my apprenticeship next month!"

"That's great!" you say. Now your best friend can join you and Ahsoka as Padawans. With many battles yet to come in the Clone Wars, perhaps the three of you will have a chance to fight together. Or perhaps your paths will take you each to the opposite corners of the galaxy. No matter what happens, you know that you will always be connected by the power of the Force, and by the ties of friendship.

THE END

"Bitt Panith will still be there *after* we've rescued Master Eerin," you chide.

Quickly you make your way back to the site of the beacon.

"Argo," you instruct your droid, "hack into the freighter's computer and see if you can find where they're keeping Master Eerin."

R3-G0 ejects from the starfighter and wheels his way to the nearest comm terminal. *"Bip beep bzurp!"* the astromech droid beeps excitedly.

"He's found her!" you translate.

You bolt down the corridor with Jaylen right at your heels. At the door to the holding cells you press the control panel, opening the door with a *whoosh*. Something's wrong; the holding cells are empty.

"Another trap!" Jaylen says.

He's right, you think. You can sense a powerful presence behind you. Relying on your Jedi reflexes to save you, you grab your lightsaber and spin around to face your adversary . . .

Turn to page 91.

Panith has a head start, but you are younger and faster than he is. You catch up with him just as he's about to climb into his escape shuttle.

"So you abandoned your companions?" the scientist says.

"I didn't abandon them," you reply. "They can handle your monster, and you're no match for me."

"Ah, but I am not alone," Panith says with a sneer. Out from his ship appears a MagnaGuard. "And a Jedi without the Force is no match for my bodyguard."

That's right, the Force! Now that you are away from Krossen, the power of the Force surges through your body, making you feel whole again. Your lightsaber flashes to life and in one deft swing you slice Panith's droid in half.

Suddenly you hear a thumping explosion coming from the direction of the laboratory. Lights flicker in the hallway. Something must have happened to your friends!

Turn to page 60.

"We're going to Kashyyyk," you say. "Master Eerin wants me to find this Crovan guy, and that's exactly what I intend to do."

"But all we have to go on is a name. How can we possibly find one man on a planet that size?" Jaylen asks.

"Simple," you reply. "We ask the Wookiees for help. They've been friends to the Jedi for thousands of years." It's not much of a plan, but it will have to do for now.

You set your ship down at the spaceport of Kashyyyk's Royal City, home of King Grakchawwaa. This place, like all Wookiee villages, is built high in the branches of the wroshyr trees. You marvel at these trees that are as tall and wide as the skyscrapers back on Coruscant. "I hope the king will see us on such short notice," you worry.

Turn to page 64.

Suddenly the tri-fighters on your tail explode into a million pieces of scrap. The incoming ship is a Republic gunship!

Your radio comes to life as the clone pilot calls in. "Captain Herc here," the comforting clone voice says. "You're all clear, Commander. The Eighteenth Battalion has your back."

Herc's gunship is not alone. You see three more behind him, each loaded with clone troopers and assault vehicles. It appears this mission just went from an investigation to all-out war!

"General Eerin is waiting for you at the forward command center," Herc says. "If you'll just follow me, Commander, we'll make sure there are no further interruptions."

General Eerin? So your new Jedi Master is safe and sound on the planet's surface. Now you'll get to see firsthand how a Jedi fights on the battlefield!

Turn to page 35.

You quickly secure Bitt Panith to make sure he can't escape and then sprint back toward the laboratory, fearing the worst. The explosion sounded massive, but you don't smell smoke or see any damage aside from the flickering lights.

Inside the laboratory, you are relieved to see Jaylen and Sergeant Lex completely unharmed. They're standing over Krossen, who has collapsed in a pile on the floor. "Thank goodness you guys are safe!" you cry. "I thought I heard an explosion."

"You did, sort of," Jaylen says. "It was Lex's idea. He used an electromagnetic pulse bomb to fry that cyborg's circuits. Parts of him might still be alive, but without his mechanical components, he's as useless as a starship without an engine."

"That was brilliant, Sergeant!" you say. So that explains the flickering lights. The EMP bomb must have shorted out all of the electronics in range. Suddenly you remember R3-G0. "Argo?"

The little astromech droid doesn't respond. On closer inspection, you notice smoke coming from beneath his dome. The damage looks pretty serious.

Sergeant Lex places a comforting hand on your shoulder. "He was a very brave little droid,

Commander. I'll help you carry him back to the ship."

The three of you, with your prisoner and droid in tow, return to the forward command center where Master Eerin waits for you with pride. "I see the mission was a success, my Padawan. Let us return to Coruscant so that this criminal can stand trial." Seeing your concern for the disabled droid, Eerin adds, "And so that we can attend to the needs of our friends."

Turn to page 125.

"Jaylen, can you get us right above the cockpit of that ship? Close enough so I can see inside?"

"I think so," Jaylen says. "But only for a few seconds at most."

"Good enough." Jaylen rotates the ship into position, then releases the accelerator, causing the bounty hunter's ship to speed up relative to your starfighter until he's directly underneath you. At the last second, Jaylen speeds up so that the two ships are speeding through space in sync. You focus your senses in the moment so that time seems to slow to a crawl around you. You peer down into the bounty hunter's cockpit, where you can see the Trandoshan pilot hissing in anger. But that's not what you're after. You peer closer at the ship's control panel. When you see the accelerator switch, you raise your hand and imagine yourself pulling it down to full throttle, twisting it so tight that the metal lever jams in position. With the power of the Force, it's as if your hand is there inside the enemy's ship, making it happen. It works! Suddenly time snaps back into its proper speed. As you watch the Trandoshan fighter speed off into the distance, your Force-enhanced hearing can just make out the pilot shouting, "Jedi poodoo!"

"We've seen the last of him," you say proudly. "That ship isn't stopping till it runs out of fuel or crashes into an asteroid."

"We make quite a team, don't we?" Jaylen grins. "Let's take out that lab. Just the two of us! We can't stop now!"

If you continue on to the research facility, turn to page 27.

If you go back to check on Master Eerin now that the trap is sprung, turn to page 56.

No sooner have you stepped out of your starfighter than you are approached by a very official-looking Wookiee. "Come with me at once, Jedi. King Grakchawwaa wishes to see you," the Wookiee roars in the animal-like Shyriiwook language. (It's a good thing you chose to take Shyriiwook as your language elective during your training, you think.)

"I guess we don't have to worry about getting an audience after all!" Jaylen says.

The Wookiee emissary leads you over rope bridges and up hand-cranked elevators to the throne room. King Grakchawwaa does not look happy . . .

"Who does Quaagan think he is?!" the mighty Wookiee roars. "I, Grakchawwaa, am the rightful king!"

"Great and powerful Grakchawwaa," you say. "Your leadership is not in doubt with the Jedi. That is why we came to you for aid. We are looking for a man named Crovan Dane. Perhaps you've heard of him?"

"Raaagh! I care not about this man. Quaagan is my enemy! He could not oppose me at the tribal council, so now he plots with Separatists to steal my throne!" Separatists here on Kashyyyk? This could be trouble. King Grakchawwaa continues, "I cannot attack him directly without risking a tribal war, but you, Jedi . . . you can stop him!"

"Do you have proof that he is working with the Separatists, your Highness?" you ask.

"Proof? Proof does not matter! Will you honor our friendship, Jedi, and fight my enemy?"

If you stick the mission and look for Crovan, turn to page 73.

If you agree to assist King Grakchawwaa, turn to page 134.

"All right, we surrender," you say as you lay down your lightsaber. Jaylen clearly isn't pleased with your call, but he follows your lead nonetheless.

The compound door opens and a pair of MagnaGuards emerge, their electrostaffs ready to slice you in half if you try to escape. They escort you into the facility where you are each placed in separate holding cells. From behind bars you can see Muun scientists going about their research, barely giving you a passing glance. You've never felt so powerless.

After what feels like hours, your captor reveals himself at last. Doctor Bitt Panith wears a lab coat and surgical mask that are stained with some sort of fluid. It could be blood or hydraulic fluid—you'll never know.

"Two Jedi students. How good of you to join us. You're just in time for the final stages of my project. Krossen, my masterpiece, is ready to test on a live subject." Doctor Panith scratches his chin and then points at Jaylen. "You'll do nicely, youngling."

"Wait!" you interrupt. "You promised not to hurt us!"

"No," Doctor Panith corrects, "I said I would not hurt you as long as I live and breathe." The Muun

cientist pulls back his lab coat to reveal a cybernetic
body attached to his perfectly organic head and hands.
He's a cyborg! "Technically speaking, I *don't* breathe. Ha
ha ha!"

Doctor Panith and his MagnaGuards escort Jaylen
through a large reinforced door. "Don't worry, young
Padawan," Panith tells you. "We'll be back for you soon
enough!"

Turn to page 119.

"Master Eerin, with your permission I would like to lead the strike squad, but on one condition."

Bant Eerin looks at you curiously. "Yes, Padawan?"

"I want to take Jaylen with me," you say. "If I won't have you to guide me, then I want someone I trust watching my back."

"Very well. I am placing the youngling under your care." Eerin motions toward a clone trooper with purple markings. "Sergeant Lex here is our demolition expert. Locked doors, no matter how thick, are no match for his explosives. I also suggest you take along your astromech droid."

Argo? you think. You just hope that patchwork of wires doesn't malfunction when you need him!

With your team assembled, you make your way toward Bitt Panith's secret base. You cross your fingers that Master Eerin's assault on Panith's droid forces will distract the scientist from your presence long enough for you to sneak inside.

So far, so good. You have the entrance in your sights. And, as luck would have it, there appear to be minimal defenses—just a pair of bumbling battle droids. "Roger, roger," you hear them chirp to each other. This will be all too easy.

You and Jaylen look at each other and grin. "I've got the one on the left," you say.

Moving as one, the two of you leap out from behind your cover and each grab one of the battle droids remotely with the power of the Force. Before the flustered sentries can react, you and Jaylen wave your arms, slamming the droids into each other. They're nothing but scrap metal now.

With the coast clear, Argo wheels up to the locked door and hacks through the security codes. The door opens with a *whoosh*. You're in!

Turn to page 98.

The Jedi Council gives you a day to get your mind in order before summoning you for a report. You take the turbolift to the top of the spire where the Council convenes. As you step into the circle, you see many familiar faces: Jedi Masters who are legendary in the Jedi Order. You regret that you could not meet them under better circumstances.

The first question comes from Kit Fisto. "What of my former Padawan, Bant Eerin? Did you find her?" he asks. Famous for his cheerful visage, Fisto isn't smiling now.

"No, Master Fisto. I never found her. I think she was captured by bounty hunters . . . I didn't investigate."

Next to question you is Mace Windu, who has only just returned from a costly battle in the Outer Rim. "And Bitt Panith's secret project on Akoshissss, did you discover what he was working on?" Mace Windu asks. His piercing gaze makes you feel as small and insignificant as a gnat.

"No, Master Windu. I escaped before finding that out. He did mention something called Krossen, though."

The final and most difficult question comes from

Master Yoda. "A youngling, into battle you did take. Inform the Council, you did not. Of Jaylen Kos's fate, what have you to report?"

As you try to answer, you feel tears welling up in your eyes. How do you tell the people you most admire that you failed your best friend in the galaxy? "I . . . I left him on Akoshissss. They took him away. I couldn't . . . What was I supposed to do?"

The members of the Council deliberate on your report, leaving you standing there awkwardly as they consider punishments. Mace Windu delivers their decision. "Initiate, you are hereby stripped of the rank of Padawan. You are to return to your classes until such time as another Jedi chooses you as a Padawan . . . that is, if there is any Jedi who could trust someone who has shown such a lack of character." The words sting, especially because you know them to be true.

Perhaps it's time you considered a future *outside* the Jedi Order . . .

THE END

You push the bowl of writhing worms away. "I come to you in peace, and this is the respect you show me?" you shout.

Raikhssa leaps from his chair. "Ressspect? What do you know of ressspect, Jedi? You are the one who insssults all Trandoshans by ssspurning a finer meal than even I, the War Chief, could asssk for!"

The hall is in an uproar. Many Trandoshans hiss threats while a few bolder ones throw stones at you.

"If you will not hear me out," you say, "then I'll be on my way . . ."

Raikhssa screams at you. "You! The only place you will go, Jedi, isss to the ssspice mines of Kessel!"

A hulking pair of Trandoshan guards block your exit. Before you can pull out your lightsaber for some "aggressive negotiations," a Trandoshan slaver blasts you with his stun rifle. Everything goes black.

You wake up to find yourself chained up in a dark cave. A gruff Trandoshan guard throws you a rusty shovel and barks, "Get to work, ssslave!" To think that your fortunes could change so drastically over a bowl of worms . . .

THE END

This sounds like a local dispute to you. Certainly a Jedi could help in negotiations, but right now you have a more pressing concern than helping a paranoid Wookiee chieftain. "I am sorry, your Highness, but I have to find Crovan Dane. I will tell the Council of your troubles and see that you receive the assistance you ask for."

Now that you've turned him down, the Wookiee king is not very eager to help you on your mission. You have a strong sense that none of his people are interested in helping you for fear of offending their leader. "I guess we'll have to find Crovan on our own," you say. "Any ideas on where to start our search?"

"How about the spaceport?" Jaylen suggests. "If he's got a starship, he must have passed through there."

"Good thinking," you agree. Back to the spaceport you go.

Turn to page 75.

"Go ahead, Jaylen," you say. "Just try to keep the ship in one piece."

As you and Jaylen switch places, you know you made the right choice. The bounty hunter unleashes blast after blast, but Jaylen dodges every shot. It is as if the ship is an extension of his body. He doesn't even need R3-G0's assistance!

"This guy's about as maneuverable as a bantha, but he's got us outgunned," Jaylen says. "Sooner or later he's going to get a shot in, and when that happens, we're space scrap."

"I've got a plan," you assure him.

Turn to page 62.

The Kashyyyk spaceport is filled with merchants and travelers from across the galaxy. There are Wookiees, of course, and Trandoshans, humans, Twi'leks, and other species you've never seen before.

Jaylen gives you a nudge and points across the crowds to where a Neimoidian diplomat with MagnaGuard escorts is preparing to board a transport. "He must be with the Trade Federation, and an important guy, too, if he has MagnaGuards with him. We'd better keep a low profile," you say as you pull your hood up to cover your Padawan braid.

You ask around, but no one you talk to has heard of Crovan Dane. Or at least no one admits to it. You have a feeling some of them are lying.

Just when you are about to give up your search, you are approached by a shady-looking Toydarian mechanic. "Well, well, my young friends! I couldn't help but overhear that you are looking for Crovan Dane," the Toydarian says, flapping his tiny wings to keep aloft. "I might know such a man. But there are so many faces, so many names . . . Maybe a few credits could get my memory working."

You do have a few hundred Republic credits for an emergency you could offer him.

Suddenly you hear a roar coming from the Neimoidian's ship. It looks like the MagnaGuards are trying to force a young Wookiee onto the ship against her will. If you act now, you might be able to intervene. On the other hand, two untried Jedi initiates don't stand much of a chance against those MagnaGuards.

The Toydarian notices your attention swaying and says, "Look, I'm a busy man. If you aren't interested in quality information, I'll take my business elsewhere."

If you confront the Neimoidian about his Wookiee prisoner, turn to page 145.

If you stay and pay the Toydarian, turn to page 105.

With the scientist's ship set to explode and his MagnaGuards scrapped, you set off to capture Doctor Panith himself. When you enter the laboratory, you find Panith hunched over a large workbench, furiously tinkering with his cyborg creation.

"What are you doing here?" Panith asks, too absorbed in his work to turn around. "Krossen isn't ready yet. I told you to wait at the ship!"

"About your ship, it's not leaving Akoshissss anytime soon," you tell the cyberneticist. Panith spins around to see who's invaded his laboratory. "Show him, Sergeant."

Sergeant Lex presses the button on a portable detonator. The entire compound shakes from the explosion of Panith's ship.

"Jedi!" Panith yells. "You've crossed the wrong scientist. MagnaGuards, kill the intruders!"

You ignite your lightsaber and walk toward your panicking target. "It's over, Panith," you say. "Your guards are gone. Outside, our clone army has crushed your droid defenses. We're shutting Project Krossen down and you're coming back to Coruscant with us."

"I'll never surrender to you, Jedi," Panith says as he draws a blaster from beneath his lab coat and points it right at you. You don't have time to react.

"Watch out!" Jaylen calls. Before Doctor Panith can fire, Jaylen reaches out and grabs the blaster from across the room with the power of the Force. His last defense gone, Panith is forced to surrender. "Bet you're happy you brought me along." Jaylen smiles.

"Don't get cocky, Jaylen. You're still a youngling," you tease. "Let's take this criminal back to Master Eerin. I don't know about you, but I'm ready to go home."

Turn to page 33.

You stare at Gama Bankor with the piercing look you remember your Jedi teachers giving you when you used to get in trouble back at the Temple. "We may be young," you say, "but our Masters are more powerful than you could ever imagine and they'll be here any minute."

Gama Bankor stares into your eyes as if searching for signs of deception, but ultimately decides it isn't worth the risk to find out. "Droids, release the Wookiee. The trip home will be far more pleasant without her stinking up the ship anyway."

As one of the MagnaGuards undoes her shackles, the Wookiee roars defiantly in the droid's face. "ROOOAR!" She may be young, but this Wookiee has guts!

"Come! Let us be rid of this forsaken overgrown garden." And with that, the Neimoidian diplomat is gone.

Your bluff worked!

Turn to page 22.

As you and Jaylen hurry toward the garden, you catch a glimpse of the Jedi war rooms.

"Hey! I think I see Mace Windu!" Jaylen says. "Maybe I'll be assigned to him. I'd make a great Padawan for him!"

"Be serious," you chide him. "Even if that was Master Windu, he's too *important* to take on a Padawan right now."

As remote a possibility as it is, you can't help but imagine what it would be like to train one-on-one with such an amazing teacher. Before the Clone Wars took hold of the galaxy, the halls of the Jedi Temple were full of Padawans who would return for lessons between assignments. Now, Padawans get their training on the battlefield. Being promoted to Padawan isn't like an apprenticeship anymore; now it means becoming an adult and taking all of the burdens of the adult world on your shoulders. "Hurry up," you say to Jaylen, picking up the pace. "We're almost to the garden."

Turn to page 151.

If you don't do something, who knows what that mad scientist will do to your best friend! Before fear sinks in, you take off in pursuit of Jaylen and his captors. You run through the reinforced doors and down a maze of corridors until you find yourself in a large operating room where the fiendish Doctor Panith is strapping Jaylen onto a gurney. A surgical droid uses sticky electrodes to hook the boy up to an imposing medical scanner, while various humanoid assistants look on. You hide behind a surgical console, staying perfectly still and taking shallow breaths so as not to be noticed.

"As you can see, the subject shows typical midi-chlorian activity for a Jedi of his age," Doctor Panith explains to his attentive assistants. "Now let us see how he responds to *subject XK-7*."

A pair of doors wide enough to fly a starfighter through swing open and another gurney is wheeled in. Strapped to the slab is a hulking hybrid of monster and metal: *Krossen*. His face is still vaguely reptilian, but the rest of his body has been altered beyond recognition. If the holo-images you've seen of General Grievous showed a cyborg built for speed and finesse, Krossen is a cyborg built purely for brute strength. This is the secret weapon to be used against the Jedi?

Doctor Panith returns to his demonstration. "As you know, the key to Project Krossen is the transfusion of Force-resistant terentatek blood into a cyborg host. Subjects XK-1 through XK-6 rejected the blood, but XK-7 appears stable." The mad Muun scientist checks Jaylen's readings before continuing. "Ah! The subject shows a ninety percent drop in midi-chlorian activity. Now we only need to confirm his abilities in a combat environment."

So that's Panith's plan: a *Force-resistant* cyborg! You let out a gasp . . . Oops!

Too late. All eyes turn on you. "I see we have a *volunteer*," Doctor Panith says with a sinister sneer. The last thing you remember before blacking out is a MagnaGuard fist swinging toward your head.

Turn to page 19.

Sunchoo leads you down into the Shadowlands of Kashyyyk. After several hours of marching, Sunchoo stops you and points to a faint light in the distance. "There's his camp," she growls.

Following Sunchoo's lead, you creep up to the edge of the camp and get your first look at the man Master Eerin sent you to apprehend. To call Crovan Dane rough would be an understatement. His skin is rugged and scarred and from his belt hang a pair of modified blaster pistols. And he's not alone; his partner is a gray-haired Wookiee with a metal patch over one eye. If anything, this furry fellow looks even more dangerous than Crovan.

"What kind of Wookiee would sell his own kind into slavery?" Jaylen asks.

"A very dangerous one," Sunchoo responds.

Turn to page 90.

Back at the forward command center you are greeted by the cheers of hundreds of clone troopers. Only twenty-four hours ago you were just a youngling who had never experienced combat outside of simulations, and now here you are, the hero of the Battle of Akoshissss.

One clone trooper isn't cheering. You recognize him as Sergeant Troy, the same soldier who questioned you command. He takes off his helmet and strides toward you, a steely look in his eye. "You've got a lot of nerve rookie, ordering us around like that . . ."

Uh-oh!

". . . but you've got the guts and the brains to back it up. It was an honor to serve under you, Commander." Sergeant Troy takes your hand and shakes it with admiration.

In these Clone Wars there are many battles yet to come, but after your experiences today, you are ready to do your part to win them so that peace can be restored to the galaxy once and for all.

THE END

"This isn't the time for you to prove yourself, Jaylen," you say. "I can handle this!"

The bounty hunter's ship is closing in, laser cannons blazing. You grip the flight-stick of your Delta-7B and pull back sharply to outmaneuver the bounty hunter's ship, but your enemy is too quick. "I can't shake him!" The laser blasts get closer.

You hear a mechanical wail and see sparks flying from the port wing. "I've lost Argo!"

With your astromech droid out of commission, you don't notice the torpedoes until it's too late. "Brace for impact!" you yell. There's no explosion from the hit, though. These are EMP torpedoes, designed to take out your ship's electrical circuits with an electromagnetic pulse. You can feel the *thoomp* of the EMP blast. Your ship is now utterly powerless.

The bounty hunter uses a tractor beam to tow you back to the cargo hold of the freighter. Through your cockpit window you can see your adversary approaching. It's a young Trandoshan bounty hunter in an orange flight suit, and right now he's got a blaster pointed at you. "Out of the ssship, Jedi ssscum!"

"Just do what he says," you tell Jaylen as you open the cockpit and slowly make your exit. "If he wanted us dead, he would have just shot down our ship."

"Toss me lightsssabers, younglingsss!" the Trandoshan hisses. You and Jaylen have no choice but to comply. You throw him your lightsabers, which were your last defense. "Yesss . . . three lightsssabers in one day!"

Three? He must have Master Eerin's, too! "What do you want with us, lizard lips? Who hired you?!"

"Hired? Bossk not hired. Bossk not bounty hunter yet. But with these lightsssabers, Guild will surely let Bossk in. Now, go join your Massster . . . in death! *Ssshak ssshak ssshak!*" You've never heard a more unpleasant sound than the Trandoshan's laugh, but it's the last sound you'll ever hear.

THE END

One unarmed Padawan against all these Separatist
forces? Those are not odds you want to gamble your
life on. Everyone is so focused on whatever Doctor
Panith is doing behind those doors, you manage to slip
out of the compound and back to your ship without
being seen. Soon you'll be back in the safety of the Jedi
Temple and you can put this nightmare behind you . . .

Turn to page 70.

You swallow your fear and say to Jaylen, "Now we have to act like Jedi."

"But what can the two of us do against a Sith-trained assassin?" Jaylen asks.

"I've got a plan," you reply with a smile.

After explaining your plan to Jaylen, you sprint toward Ventress by yourself. You grip the hilt of your lightsaber, a weapon that has never been used outside of the training room in the Jedi Temple. Will it be enough to keep you alive against Ventress's twin blades?

Now is the time to find out. With a flick of your wrist, you ignite your lightsaber and leap into the air. Sensing your approach, she turns toward you and connects her two lightsaber hilts to form a single deadly double-bladed lightsaber. You bring your blade down hard, hoping to sever her lightsaber before she can swing it . . .

Too late! Ventress's reflexes are faster than yours. She dodges your attack and swings at your feet. Instead of a graceful landing, you stumble across the rocky ground, ripping your robes and scraping up your knees.

Ventress stands above you, ready to deal a finishing

low, when suddenly a powerful voice rings out across he barren moon. "Get away from my Padawan!" Master Eerin arrived just in time!

You jump to your feet and take position beside your Master. Even though the two of you have never fought ogether before, you quickly adapt to each other's moves. As a synchronized fighting force, you and Bant Eerin are venly matched against Dooku's protégé. Lights flare as our blades clash, but no one gets hit.

You become so caught up in the battle, you almost ail to notice the worker droids who are hauling an normous crate from the underground facility toward Ventress's ship. That must be Bitt Panith's secret weapon! Master Eerin has noticed it, too. "If Ventress escapes vith that crate, it will lead to the death of many Jedi," erin says.

Turn to page 135.

From your hiding place, you watch as Crovan and Tahnchukka load their ship with cages containing strange and savage creatures. There's even a family of Wookiees!

"It won't be long now, Tank. We've got everything on Panith's list, including his terentatek," Crovan says

So that's why Master Eerin sent you here! Crovan Dane is collecting creatures for use in Bitt Panith's cyborg research. Something about the name terentatek sounds familiar, but you can't quite place it . . .

Suddenly Tahnchukka stops in his tracks and sniffs the air. He's heading in your direction!

"What is it, Tank?" Crovan asks.

You take hold of your lightsaber and silently motion to Jaylen. But before you can step out to confront the Wookiee mercenary, Sunchoo grabs your arm. "Wait! Stay where you are. It's me he smells," she whispers. "If I turn myself in, it will buy you time."

If you listen to Sunchoo and remain hidden, turn to page 39.

If you confront Crovan, turn to page 101.

You find yourself face-to-face with an imposing Mon Calamari female, dressed in the robes of a Jedi Knight. It's Master Bant Eerin!

"I hope you aren't planning to use that lightsaber against me," she says with a smile.

"Forgive me, Master Eerin," you say. "We're here to rescue you." Although by the looks of things, Bant Eerin seems to have done just fine escaping on her own.

"That was very brave of you, young ones." Bant shifts her gaze to Jaylen. "But I don't remember Master Yoda mentioning a *second* Padawan."

You tell Bant Eerin everything.

"This is a very serious matter, youngling Jaylen Kos, and you will have to answer for your disobedience when we return to the Jedi Temple," Bant says to your friend. "That said, you are here for the duration of the mission. Because of the delay caused by the bounty hunter, we can't afford to waste another minute. Follow me to Panith's base." You and Jaylen nod affirmatively. "And young ones, no more surprises."

Turn to page 120.

You know you only have a few seconds before Crovan and his Wookiee henchman come back.

"Open all the cages," you tell Jaylen. "And be careful; some of these creatures look like they haven't been fed in days."

Carefully, you begin to release the trapped creatures. On the other side of the camp, Jaylen is doing the same.

There's only one cage left. This one is larger than all the others and has walls as thick as blast doors. Whatever is in there must be incredibly strong. You hit the switch to open the cage, but before you can see what's inside, a voice calls out from inside the ship. "What in Mustafar's fires is going on out there?!"

Suddenly Crovan spots you and Jaylen among the beasts. "Hands up, whoever you are! Any sudden movements, and I'll fire."

Turn to page 122.

If it's a fight Jaylen wants, then it's a fight you'll give him. Maybe when he's faced the humiliation of defeat, he'll finally come to his senses. "You think you can take me, Jaylen? Let's settle this now," you say.

You motion to the men under your command to keep their distance. Asajj Ventress grins wickedly and shows no interest in intervening.

You and Jaylen approach each other, lightsabers glowing brightly. Like tigers preparing for the kill, the two of you prowl in a circle, sizing each other up. Back at the Temple, you and Jaylen sparred many times before, but that was in a classroom—this time, it's for real.

Jaylen strikes first. He lunges at you with an overhead swing. You block effortlessly, but Jaylen is strong and his strike knocks you backward. A quick glance reminds you that you are hundreds of feet up in the air. A misstep in that direction and you'll fall to certain death. While you are distracted, Jaylen swings again, grazing your shoulder and drawing blood. A surge of anger washes through your body.

Now it's your turn to attack. You swing your green blade low at Jaylen's feet, causing him to jump backward, exactly as you want him to. Now you follow up with a quick set of blows, which Jaylen deflects easily enough, but he's starting to tire.

You feign an opening, daring Jaylen to make the next move. He takes the bait, swinging at you hard. Big mistake. You leap into the air and somersault over Jaylen. While his back is turned, you hit him with a solid kick.

The blow was only meant to stun your opponent, but you must have hit him harder than you intended. Suddenly Jaylen is staggering backward, toward the cliff face. You watch in horror as your best friend tumbles over the edge.

"Jaylen!" you scream as you run toward him. But it's too late. Jaylen is gone.

Turn to page 44.

You dash across the battlefield on foot, narrowly dodging incoming blasts from the droid forces. Through the shimmering energy shield you go. Now you're safe from blasts from the outside. You can see the shield generator straight ahead, but standing in front of you is a row of droidekas, or destroyer droids. Great, you think, shields within shields!

As the droidekas open fire, you realize that you're going to need help to reach the generator. Scanning your surroundings you see a lone clone trooper holding his own against the onslaught of droids. You recognize that clone with the red shoulder armor. It's Sergeant Troy, the soldier who has been giving you grief ever since you took command.

Sergeant Troy looks your way and scoffs. "Well, if it isn't the little general."

It takes great effort to keep your anger checked as you respond, "Sergeant, I need your help."

"Oh, I can help you," the defiant clone says. "But *this time*, we're doing things my way, rookie."

Turn to page 124.

Sunchoo leads you back to her village, where you and Jaylen are treated to a hero's welcome. The rescued Wookiees tell stories of your bravery to their family members and each and every villager comes to thank you personally. "Let us celebrate the return of those who were lost and welcome these Jedi into our tribe!" a particularly shaggy Wookiee roars. You've never seen such a party!

As night gives way to dawn, you pull Sunchoo aside to say farewell. "I'm sorry, Sunchoo. Jaylen and I have to return to our home. There are many more battles that must be fought if peace is to return to the galaxy."

Sunchoo sniffles. "But the Life Debt . . . I must repay you for all you have done!"

"You led us to Crovan. You bravely turned yourself in to give us the distraction we needed. We could not have completed our mission without you, Sunchoo. Consider the debt paid," you say.

Sunchoo shakes her head. "I will never forget what you have done. Even if I cannot follow you, know that you only need give the word and I will cross the galaxy to come to your aid."

THE END

"I won't fight you, Jaylen," you say. "Those traitors are my enemies, but you are not." You motion to your clone troopers to advance. "Take out Ventress and the traitor Quaagan, but leave Jaylen alive."

Asajj Ventress grabs Jaylen with one hand and ignites one of her curved lightsaber hilts with the other. "This fool of a Wookiee is not worth fighting for," she says. "Come, Jaylen. You can fight your friend another day. Once I have finished training you, you will battle many Jedi."

The clone troopers fire at the assassin, but Ventress effortlessly deflects the blaster shots. With Jaylen beside her, she takes off in her ship, leaving Quaagan to deal with you and your troops alone.

You drag Quaagan back to Grakchawwaa at the Royal City. As far as the Wookiee king is concerned, the mission was a success. The challenger to the throne has been defeated.

But for you, this is no time for celebration. Jaylen is gone, lost to the temptation of the dark side. If you meet again, it will not be as friends. You hope that day never comes.

THE END

The secret facility is vast and labyrinthine. If you aren't careful, you could get lost in here.

"Where do we go now?" Jaylen asks.

"Shh! I think I hear something," you say.

"Tell Count Dooku that Project Krossen will soon be ready for transport." This voice is cold, almost metallic, but not a droid's voice. And what is this "Krossen"? Could that be the top secret project this base was built to hide?

"Yes, Doctor Panith." So that first voice must be Bitt Panith, your target!

As you peek around the corner you see Doctor Panith disappear down one corridor, while a pair of MagnaGuards exit down another.

"What are we waiting for?" Jaylen urges.

Sergeant Lex holds up a hand in warning. "Sir, I recommend caution. As long as we take out the doctor's ship, he won't be going anywhere."

If you follow the droids to the hangar, turn to page 113.

If you follow Doctor Panith to the laboratory, turn to page 48.

"I'm not leaving you, Sergeant," you say. "It's going to take all of us to bring down this monster."

Bitt Panith was wrong when he said your Jedi training wouldn't serve you. The way of the Jedi is about more than battling with a lightsaber or manipulating objects with the Force. It is about using your wits and your heart. No cyborg can take that power away from you.

"I've got a plan," you say to your team. "It's going to take all of us working together."

On your orders, Sergeant Lex starts firing on Krossen, drawing the monster toward the laboratory's main doors. R3-G0 hacks into the main computer. When the cyborg steps into the doorway, the little droid causes the doors to shut fast, momentarily trapping Krossen.

Now it's your turn. With a boost from Jaylen, you leap onto Krossen's back and manage to wrest off its mask with your bare hands. The face beneath is a blur of slime and fangs more gruesome than anything you could have imagined. If its face is from one beast or from a mix of many, you don't know. All that matters is that this is Krossen's weak spot. "Let him have it, Lex," you call out. The clone commando nods and fires a direct shot into the cyborg's gaping maw. That does the trick. Krossen falls with a mighty thud.

Bitt Panith may have escaped, but at least you know what he was up to. Whether the mission was a success or not, only time will tell. Right now, it's time to go back to your Jedi Master. It's time to go home.

Turn to page 55.

"No, Sunchoo. We can handle this. We're Jedi."
You grab your lightsaber and motion to Jaylen to
follow.

"Crovan Dane," you call out. "You are under
arrest for conspiring against the Republic. Surrender
peacefully and return with us to Coruscant."

"Or what?" Crovan scoffs as he points his blaster in
your direction.

This should be easy, you think to yourself. Two
mercenaries should be no match for two Jedi in
training. You reach out toward Crovan's blaster,
willing it out of his hand and into yours . . . and nothing
happens. What's wrong, you wonder. The Force pull is
a technique you mastered years ago!

Crovan laughs and taps the side of a large cage.
"That's right, Jedi. In this cage is a terentatek. It's one
of only a handful of creatures capable of repelling the
Force. Your powers won't serve you now."

He's right. You can't feel the Force around you at all.

"After the mess your people caused on Geonosis,
there are plenty of folks who would pay good money
for Jedi prisoners," Crovan schemes. "This is our
lucky day, eh, Tank?" The one-eyed Wookiee grunts in
agreement.

You turn to run, but it's no use. Without your Force-heightened reflexes, Crovan and his Wookiee partner are too fast for you. The last thing you remember is hearing a stun blaster go off behind you . . .

Turn to page 9.

"No caves today, Jaylen," you say. "We're taking the direct approach. Keep your eyes open for any battle droids."

You lead your best friend across the rocky expanse in the direction of the research facility. You keep your hand on the hilt of your lightsaber, expecting a droid platoon to march out at any moment, but your eyes see nothing. Finally, when you're within a hundred feet of the compound door, you pull Jaylen aside and hide behind a rock outcropping.

"Does this make sense to you?" you ask. "A top secret laboratory and zero security? Something's not right. I feel a presence out there, I just can't see it."

Jaylen scoffs. "You're imagining things. You just can't accept that we got lucky this time." Before you can plan your next move, Jaylen runs out from the cover and toward the door.

Suddenly that feeling you had starts to come into focus. "Jaylen, wait!" you call out. "It's guarded by . . ."

Chameleon droids. Dozens of them. The spider-like droids drop the holographic arrays that kept them invisible to the eye and turn their lasers on you and Jaylen.

You notice that one of the droids has a holoprojector. It skitters to within a few feet of you before activating the projector. A glowing blue hologram of a Muun scientist addresses you.

"Welcome to Akoshissss, Jedi. I am Doctor Bitt Panith . . . but then, if you came all this way, you must already know who I am. Surrender to my droids and I promise you, no harm will come to you as long as I live and breathe."

If you try to fight off the droids, turn to page 25.
If you lay down your lightsaber and surrender, turn to page 66.

You reach into your bag and pull out a handful of credits. "The name again was Crovan Dane. Ring any bells?" you ask as you wave the credits in front of the Toydarian's face.

The Toydarian's eyes light up. "Oh, yes! Crovan, of course! He's a very dangerous man, you know. A smuggler! He's down in the Shadowlands now. What his business is down there, I couldn't say."

"Will you take us to him?" Jaylen asks.

"Me, go to the Shadowlands?" the Toydarian says incredulously. "Not a chance! But I know someone who can help you. Someone else who is looking for this Crovan. He will lead you right to him!"

"Very well. Take us to him," you say.

The Toydarian leads you down a series of ramps to the lowest level of the Wookiee village. Up ahead is a sleazy-looking cantina. "In there. Ask for Goomi. Tell him Zaboshka sent you," the mechanic says. "Oh, and I should warn you—Goomi is a *shapeshifter*, and he's quite fond of jokes."

Turn to page 140.

You have seen cyborgs before. Usually, they resemble their original forms, with the mechanical bits merely enhancing or replacing an organic function. There are some cyborgs, like the nefarious General Grievous, who are more machine than living being, but they are still quite rare in the galaxy. Krossen is entirely different. He (or is it an "it"?) is cobbled together from parts of various creatures, great and small. His massive arms look like they came from a gundark, one of the strongest beasts in the galaxy. His legs are as sturdy as those of a gamorrean. As for his face, it is hidden behind a terrifying metal mask. Armor plates and hidden weaponry are built into the thing's body. But this monster hides another secret. Something doesn't feel right. Beside you, Jaylen trembles in his Jedi robes. In all your years of friendship, you've never seen him like this. He's afraid. You feel a wave of nausea pass through you.

"Something's definitely wrong," you say. "I feel like a part of me is fading away."

The fiendish Doctor Panith is rubbing his hands together with glee. "I see you have discovered the Krossen's greatest power: Force immunity! The blood that runs through his veins comes from a terentatek, one of only a handful of species in the entire galaxy with a natural resistance to the Force. Your Jedi training cannot save you now."

Krossen lumbers toward you with increasing speed as his circuits come to life. The whole room shakes with each of his steps. Without the Force to guide you, what will you do?!

Turn to page 52.

You try to think back. Didn't you know Jaylen from your first day as a youngling? That certainly sounds right . . .

"You on the left, you're the real Jaylen, right?"

The "Jaylen" you picked suddenly morphs before your eyes from a Zabrak to a bluish reptilian form that you've never seen before. "Hoo hoo, what fun! I've outsmarted a Jedi," says the creature that you assume must be Goomi. "Although with a memory like that, this must not be a very bright Jedi."

The real Jaylen gives you a surly glare.

The shapeshifter says, "You are looking for Crovan Dane, yes? I seek him, too. He is a liar and a thief! He stole from my boss, and for that he shall pay! Let us go at once, little Jedi. Fool that you are, just do as I say."

You want to stick up for yourself, but after the mistake you just made, you decide to keep your mouth shut and follow along.

Turn to page 17.

With a hundred Trandoshan eyes looking your way, you take the bowl of blood worms and pour its writhing contents back into your mouth. *Crunch* go the worms as you grind them between your teeth. (As disgusting as they taste as they pop in your mouth, you hate to think of the worms still squirming in your stomach!)

War Chief Raikhssa smiles at you from his throne. "I am impresssed, Jedi. Mossst humansss cannot handle the finer foods of Trandoshan cuisine. Go ahead and deliver your messsage. I am lissstening!"

Now that you have the War Chief's respect, convincing him to turn a blind eye to the Jedi fighting on his nearby moon should be no problem. You remember back to your diplomacy lessons at the Jedi Temple. A good negotiator must maintain control while giving the other person confidence that they are calling the shots. Stroke their ego. Make them feel that they will leave the bargaining table with the upper hand.

"Arrogant Separatists were provoking an attack in Trandoshan space," you explain. "As we value your people's friendship, we felt it our duty to punish the Separatists for this offense." You explain about the base on Akoshissss, knowing full well that the evil Bitt

Panith probably paid Raikhssa for permission to build it there.

Raikhssa scratches his chin as he considers what you have told him. To seal the deal, you add, "We will, of course, generously compensate your Greatness for any inconvenience this minor skirmish might cause."

That was all the assurance the War Chief needed. "Do what you wisssh to the Ssseparatisssts, but make sssure you leave Akoshissss when you're through."

You've done it. You've convinced the Trandoshans to stay out of the battle!

Turn to page 149.

Sergeant Troy pats your shoulder. "At least we die as soldiers, eh, rookie?"

Suddenly, from up above, you hear the roar of approaching ships. Green laser blasts rain down on the droid forces. You look up to see a dozen gunships gliding down. Leading the charge is Jedi Master Kit Fisto. You've never been so happy to see a friendly face!

With the added reinforcements, you and your comrades make short work of the droid forces. Many lives are lost, but the Republic is victorious.

As the smoke clears, you and your fellow Jedi gather to honor those who died in the battle. You make eye contact with Master Eerin for the first time since she gave you command of the ground forces. "I am sorry, Master. I let you down."

Eerin shakes her head warmly. "No, Padawan. Today you showed great bravery and humility. Every victory comes with a price. As Jedi, we must strive to learn from our mistakes and ensure that the next time the price is not as great."

THE END

You know right away that the real Jaylen is the one on the right. It wasn't until your fifth year, in lightsaber training, that you and Jaylen became best friends. Clearly the one on the left is lying.

"All right, Goomi," you say to the impostor. "Enough with the games. We need you to take us to Crovan Dane."

The shapeshifter transforms before your eyes into a blue-scaled reptilian mercenary. Is this Goomi's true form, or just another ruse?

"You seek the beast hunter, most wise and tricky Jedi?" the shapeshifter asks. "Yes, I know where Crovan hides. Take you to him, I will, for I seek him also! The swindler stole from my employer, he did. He is dangerous, yes, but not for one so clever as you, young Master."

The shapeshifter's scaly lips curl in a smile. There is something about Goomi you just don't trust. Better stay on your guard, you think as you and Jaylen follow him out of the cantina and into the forest.

Turn to page 17.

"Lex's right," you say. "Let's cut off the escape route first, then we'll come back for the good doctor."

As silently as ghosts, you and your team slip into the Separatist hangar. There you find a large transport ship with its doors open and ramp extended in anticipation of Dr. Panith's forbidden cargo.

"Commander," Sergeant Lex says. "I've got the ordinance to blow that ship to the next galaxy."

"Do it, Sergeant," you reply.

"Argo, I need you to disable their security network so we can . . ." Suddenly you realize that your astromech droid has wandered off, and he's heading right up the ramp of Panith's ship! "Argo, you stupid droid, get back here!"

"BEEP BLIP BI-DIP!" Argo chirps.

"What do you mean, we have to get on the ship? We have to blow it up!" you yell to your droid. "Come back here at once!" But it's too late; Argo is already inside the ship.

If you follow R3-GO onto the ship, turn to page 30. If you stick to the plan and set the explosives, turn to page 37.

"We're checking out the signal," you say. "That's final."

You leave the research facility behind and track the distress beacon to its source on the far side of Akoshissss. The signal appears to be emanating from a disabled cargo freighter. What's more troubling are the half dozen disabled starfighters and salvage ships that float around the freighter. Among the debris is a familiar red and white Delta-7B Aethersprite.

"A Jedi starfighter!" Jaylen exclaims.

You have R3-G0 scan the ships. "That's Master Eerin's ship all right, but there's no pilot. I am picking up faint life signs from the freighter . . . I can't tell if it's her. We're going to have to dock with the ship to find out."

"This definitely stinks of a trap," Jaylen says. "If we're not careful, we'll end up dead in the water just like Master Eerin."

"Then we'll just have to be careful," you say.

Turn to page 155.

"Master Yoda always said I had a talent for talking my way out of trouble," you say. "I should be the one to go to Trandosha."

"Then you must depart at once," your Master replies. "Be careful, Padawan. The Trandoshans are not to be trusted. Be strong, and may the Force be with you."

Back to your starfighter you go. You think about your friend Ahsoka Tano. Did she do this much traveling on her first mission? You wonder what adventures she's up to with her new Master, Anakin Skywalker. You hope this mission will be over soon so that you can return to Coruscant and trade stories with her.

It is a short flight from Akoshissss to its parent planet, Trandosha. No sooner does your ship enter Trandoshan airspace than you receive a threatening transmission. "Republic ssscum! State your busssinesss on Trandosha or we shall blow you from the sssky!"

"Not a very warm welcome, is it, Argo?" you say to your droid.

From your training, you know not to let the threat anger you. The Trandoshans' words are harsh, but they come from weakness, not strength. You must stay strong, as Master Eerin said, if you will be successful here. "Greetings," you signal. "I come on behalf of the Jedi Council to speak with your leader. We require his guidance."

There is a long pause before the Trandoshans respond. "The Jedi come to usss for guidance? Kyek kyek kyek! Very well. Hisss Highnesss, the War Chief, will sssee you."

You're off to a great start!

Turn to page 132.

You place your hand on Jaylen's shoulder, and shake your head. "This is not a fight I want any part of," you whisper. When it becomes clear that no one is coming to back Goomi up, Crovan Dane speaks up. "Jedi, huh? Let me guess—they're *invisible* Jedi?"

Goomi realizes he's in trouble now and is starting to sweat. "Th-they'll be here any minute now, and then y-you'll be sorry you ever crossed the Hutts!"

Crovan nods to his Wookiee partner. "We'll take our chances."

The pair of smugglers open fire on the blue-scaled gangster. Goomi dives behind a wroshyr trunk, dodging the blasts, then leans out and fires a shot at Crovan.

The blast hits Crovan squarely in the shoulder. "Aaagh!" he cries in pain, slumping over.

Tahnchukka roars with anger and charges Goomi at his hiding spot. Before Goomi can react, the Wookiee hits him on the head with his bowcaster, knocking him unconscious.

As you watch the Wookiee return to tend to his fallen friend, you feel some sympathy for the man you were sent to find. Perhaps there is a way for this mission to end without bloodshed.

"I'll be okay, Tank. Just get the ship up and running so we can deliver these cages to Bitt Panith and get paid," Crovan says. "Goomi wasn't the first thug Ziro the Hutt sent after us, and he sure won't be the last."

You step out from hiding and approach your injured target. "I'm afraid I can't allow you to do that."

Turn to page 21.

There is no one left in the room except for a single Ortolan janitor. With his floppy blue ears and beady little eyes, he doesn't look all that strong-willed. You've never performed a Jedi mind trick in a real world situation, but if you don't try now, you'll never get another chance.

"You will release me from the cell," you say with as much conviction as you can muster.

"I will release you from your cell," the Ortolan responds. The mind trick worked. You're free!

If you follow after Jaylen, turn to page 81.
If you try to escape the compound, turn to page 87.
If you look for a way to call for help, turn to page 12.

Following Master Eerin's lead, you set your ship down on Akoshissss several hundred meters from the Separatists' secret base. The moon is completely barren with only a thin atmosphere and temperatures near freezing. A normal human would have trouble surviving in this hostile place, but you face no difficulties thanks to your Jedi training.

Bant Eerin calls you and Jaylen close to debrief you on the situation. "As I was saying before my run-in with the bounty hunter, our mission is to apprehend a dangerous rogue scientist, Doctor Bitt Panith. According to our spies, he has been working on a new cyborg weapon to use against the Jedi."

"What can we do to assist you, Master Eerin?" you ask.

"Panith is not expecting us. It will be safer if I infiltrate the facility alone," Bant Eerin says. "You and Jaylen Kos shall stay here with the ships until I return."

"But, Master Eerin!" you say. "Surely I would be of more use by your side?"

Bant Eerin shakes her head sympathetically. "I'm sorry, Padawan, but I cannot risk leaving your young friend alone, and I cannot bring him with me. Stay here and wait for my return." Sensing your disappointment, she puts her hand on your shoulder and adds, "There will be other missions."

As Bant Eerin dashes silently off toward the secret facility, you and Jaylen settle in for a long wait. Part of you is angry at your best friend for keeping you from being by your Master's side on your very first mission, but another part of you realizes that without Jaylen's help, you might not have survived long enough to see Master Eerin at all. For now you and Jaylen keep quiet and avoid making eye contact.

Suddenly, Jaylen breaks the silence. "Over there! I see a ship landing!"

Turn to page 131.

"Do you have any idea how much money you cost me, kid?" Crovan snarls. "It took us weeks to capture all those beasts! We'll never recapture them all in time to make our delivery to Doctor Panith."

You smile at the mercenary. "You wouldn't have gotten paid anyway, Crovan. My Master is arresting Bitt Panith even as we speak. If you want to live, you'll surrender to me now and face the judgment of the Jedi for betraying the Republic."

"Jedi, huh?" Crovan sneers. "Come on, Tank, buddy. Let's show these intruders what we think about the Jedi."

Crovan raises his blaster and is about to fire, when all of a sudden, a thundering roar erupts above him and a giant toothy mouth crunches down over his head. It's a terentatek, a fearsome monster the size of a rancor. That must have been what was in the large cage you opened! You avert your eyes as the terentatek swallows Crovan whole.

Tahnchukka fires his bowcaster at the beast to avenge his fallen partner, but the laser blasts bounce harmlessly off its scaly hide. Now the beast is *really* angry! The one-eyed Wookiee takes off running into the woods with the massive terentatek in pursuit.

"Do you think the Wookiee will get away?" Jaylen asks.

"I don't know. But just in case that monster is still hungry, I don't want to stick around to find out."

You go into Crovan's cargo hold and release Sunchoo and the other Wookiee prisoners.

"Let's head back to our ship so we can update Master Eerin on our success," you say.

"I've got a better idea," Sunchoo says. "Follow me!"

Turn to page 96.

"All right," you say. "Let's try things your way."

Sergeant Troy grunts. "Good call, rookie. Now follow my lead."

With the droidekas closing in, Troy retreats back toward the shield, away from the generator.

Once your backs are to the shimmering shield, Sergeant Troy yells, "Now!" and takes off running. As the droidekas pass through the large energy shield, their own shields cut out momentarily. Right in that instant, your clone companion tosses a thermal detonator toward the unprotected droids. *Kaboom!* The droidekas are destroyed!

"Here, rookie," Troy says as he tosses you a pack of explosives. "Go plant these around the generator. I've got your back."

You nod and run back toward the generator. Using your lightsaber, you cut through the generator's power hatch, toss in the explosives, and run. *Thoom!* The generator is destroyed. The energy shield is down!

Turn to page 26.

When you arrive back at the Jedi Temple, you discover that you aren't the only Padawan returning from a first mission. "Ahsoka, is that you?" you say upon spotting your friend's face. "You'll never believe the adventure Jaylen and I had!"

Ahsoka Tano smiles, seeing the two of you again. "Unless you got barfed on by a baby Hutt, I'm not impressed." Seeing your confusion, she adds, "It's a long story."

Jaylen shuffles his feet. "The Council wants to see me. After the stunt I pulled, I wouldn't be surprised if they kick me out of the Academy."

You shake your head. "They'd be losing one heck of a Jedi if they did," you reply.

"Before I go, I just wanted to say thanks for bringing me to Panith's lab. You didn't have to, but you did. No matter what happens, we'll always have that tale to share," Jaylen says.

As your friend walks off alone toward the Jedi Council tower to face his own destiny, you take a moment to reflect on yours. You have only just begun your journey on the path of a Jedi, and already you cannot wait to take the next step. You yearn to stand by Bant Eerin's side and learn about honor, justice, and wisdom from a true Master.

But before you depart for your next mission, you have some business to attend to. "Care to join me in the engineering lounge?" you ask Ahsoka. "I've got a very brave astromech droid in desperate need of repairs."

THE END

Back on Coruscant, Crovan Dane and Tahnchukka are treated like guests of the Jedi, but you and they both know that until the Council has made its judgment, they are not free to leave. Still, at least they are safe from the Hutts. The smugglers don't look half as menacing now that they've had baths and a change of clothes.

A few days later you appear before the Council. Your new Jedi Master, Bant Eerin, stands proudly behind you.

"Found Crovan Dane, you did. Expect you to bring him back to Coruscant, we did not," Yoda says.

"Master Yoda, Crovan was most cooperative," you explain. "I sensed goodness in him. I convinced him to release the cargo he would have delivered to the Separatists with assurances that we could help grant him protection from Ziro the Hutt."

Yoda exchanges glances with the other Jedi on the Council before responding. "A threat, Ziro is no longer. Safe from his grasp, Crovan Dane is."

"Thank you, Master Yoda . . ."

"However," Yoda adds, "aid the enemies of the Republic, Crovan did. Answer for this, the smuggler must."

You don't want to see Crovan punished . . . "Master Yoda, perhaps Crovan Dane would be willing to lend his unique skills in the service of the Republic?"

Yoda agrees with your suggestion. Crovan and Tahnchukka will be granted their freedom in exchange for making deliveries for the Jedi Order.

As you leave the Council Chamber, Master Eerin pulls you aside. "Excellent work, my Padawan. You have turned a near defeat into a double victory. I see great things in your future."

"Thank you, Master," you say. "I cannot wait for our next mission!"

THE END

Within minutes the surface of Akoshissss is blazing with laser fire. Battle droids and super battle droids march across the battlefield by the hundreds while long-legged spider droids tower over them. In spite of the odds, your clone soldiers bravely charge into the fray. At the vanguard of the attack is you, the Padawan commander.

You deftly swing your lightsaber to block incoming blasts, deflecting them back at the oncoming droids. When the attacking droids get too close, you knock them back with a powerful Force push. Thanks to your Jedi training and a rush of adrenaline, you feel unstoppable!

The clone troopers, inspired by your leadership, are also faring well. Even the outspoken Sergeant Troy is falling in line. You watch as an AT-TE tank single-handedly takes down a spider droid. From up on a hill above the battlefield, clone commandos take out super battle droids from hundreds of yards away with long-range rifles. At this rate, the battle will be over before you know it!

"Thirty seconds till firing range," one of the clone tank commanders calls out. Suddenly, from out of nowhere, a barrage of rockets flies toward the

AT-TEs, taking out one of the lumbering tanks in a massive explosion. From behind enemy lines comes a pair of fast-moving wheel droids.

"Hailfire droids!" Sergeant Troy calls over the radio. "They're too fast for our tanks!"

Another barrage of missiles, another AT-TE destroyed. If this keeps up, your certain victory will turn to certain defeat!

If you tell the AT-TE to stay on the shield generator, turn to page 136.

If you tell them to focus on the hailfire droids, turn to page 20.

You take out your electrobinoculars to get a better look at the ship Jaylen spotted. From the markings, you recognize it as a Confederacy ship. You notice something else—a secret entrance to Panith's facility.

"This can't be good," you say. "What if that ship is carrying reinforcements? Master Eerin could be in for trouble."

"You heard what she said. We're too *young* to do real Jedi work," Jaylen scoffs.

The Confederacy ship has now landed and is lowering a ramp. There's someone coming out. As you zoom in on the person you see someone with pale skin decorated with black tattoos, loose-fitting black robes, and a pair of curved lightsaber hilts on her belt. "That's Asajj Ventress!" you say. "She's Count Dooku's personal assassin!"

Jaylen turns to you for guidance. "What do we do now?"

If you stay by the ship and wait for Master Eerin's return, turn to page 6.

If you go after Ventress, turn to page 88.

The Trandoshan capital of Hsskhor is a slimy metropolis of metal and mud. Its busy streets are filled with mercenaries, slavers, and other unsavory sorts. This is no place for a young human, Jedi or not.

When you land your ship at the War Chief's palace, you are greeted by a surly crew of Trandoshan guards. You wonder if they are here for your safety or to intimidate you; probably both, you decide. One of the guards, a particularly grizzled brute with a metal patch bolted over one eye, beckons you to follow him. "Thisss way, Jedi. War Chief Raikhssa isss not one to be kept waiting."

Through the enormous stone doors you go, past statues of ancient warriors, to the War Chief's throne room. As you approach Raikhssa, who sits on a towering throne, you feel like a criminal on trial. Various Trandoshan officials stare down at you, muttering to one another with their snakelike tongues.

"Mighty Raikhssa, I come as an ambassador of the Jedi Council with an important message."

"Why the russsh, Jedi?" Raikhssa hisses. "You look tired and hungry. Pleassse accept thisss humble meal. I hope you will find it . . . appetizing."

Raikhssa claps his hands and a scrawny

Trandoshan slave steps forward with a large bowl. Is it just your imagination or are the contents of the bowl moving? As you get a closer look, you see that you were right—the bowl is filled with squirming Doshan blood worms! You've tasted many strange foods in your days, but never a meal that looks like it would rather be eating you!

Sensing your discomfort, Raikhssa and his fellow Trandoshans begin to laugh. "Kyek kyek kyek! What isss wrong, Jedi? Not hungry?"

Is this all some kind of joke, you wonder? Or worse, are they trying to poison you?

If you decline the blood worms, turn to page 72.
If you eat the blood worms, turn to page 109.

Your search for Crovan Dane will have to wait. If you turn down Grakchawwaa's request for aid, you risk hurting the Jedi Order's relations with the Wookiees. You cannot allow that to happen.

"Great Grakchawwaa, of course we will help you with this most important matter," you assure him. "I will send for reinforcements at once."

Your speech appears to have impressed the proud Wookiee king. "I am pleased to see that the Jedi still honor our friendship," he roars in Shyriiwook. "While I cannot join you myself, I shall send one of my strongest warriors to assist you. Chewbacca, come forward!"

A towering brown Wookiee with a bandolier strapped across his chest steps out from the crowd.

"Chewbacca will guide you to the traitor Quaagan's fortress," Grakchawwaa says.

Your own Wookiee guide and bodyguard. What a stroke of luck!

Turn to page 46.

Asajj Ventress attacks with newfound savagery, driving you and Master Eerin away from the crate. "You cannot win this battle, Jedi," the assassin says with a sneer. "Once I deliver Panith's weapon to Count Dooku, the Jedi will fall."

"Do you mean the weapon in that crate over there that's about to be crushed flatter than a sheet of carbonite?" you say.

"What?!" Ventress swings around to see your Jedi starfighter hovering above her precious cargo.

You can see Jaylen waving from the starfighter as he eases off on the repulsorlifts, smashing the crate and the worker droids who were carrying it.

Her mission failed, Ventress retreats to her ship. "You have not heard the end of this, Jedi!"

She's getting away! You are about to bolt after Ventress when Bant Eerin says, "Let her go, Padawan. Our mission is a success. Do not spoil this victory by sacrificing your life now."

"Do you think we'll see her again?" you ask.

"You can count on it, Padawan," she replies. "And next time, she won't get away from us so easily!"

THE END

"Those guys are too maneuverable," you call to the troops. "All AT-TEs, stay focused on the shield generator—*I'll* handle the hailfire droids."

Up ahead you see a battle droid speeding across the rocky field on a STAP. Quick as a comet, you sprint toward the flying machine and leap through the air, somersaulting over the pilot. With the coordination that only a Jedi can know, you manage to slice the droid pilot in two with your lightsaber and grab control of the STAP in a single motion.

You're more maneuverable than the hailfire droids. Sure, they're armed with enough guns and rockets to take down an army, but you have one advantage that no weapon can overcome: You wield the Force!

Whoosh! You fly the STAP straight for the hailfire droids, zigging and zagging through enemy fire. The blasters on your flier are no match for the hailfire's armor, but you have another plan for taking down the droid. At the last second you perform a backflip off the STAP, sending your stolen vehicle straight into the hailfire droid like a guided rocket. *Kaboom!*

One down, one to go. The other hailfire droid spins your way and locks on to you with its array of missiles. Just as it's about to fire, you use the Force to fling a battle droid into the missiles' path, causing both droids to explode in a ball of fire.

With the hailfire droids out of the way, the AT-TEs have no trouble taking out the shield generator. You hear a familiar clone voice through your comm radio as mighty Republic gunships zoom overhead. "Excellent work, Commander," Captain Herc says. "We'll take it from here."

The remaining droid forces are no match for the Republic gunships. Victory is yours!

Turn to page 84.

You follow Jaylen through the busy spaceport and down the wooden ramps of the Wookiee city. "Jaylen, slow down!" you call out. "Let's talk!" But your friend ignores you and picks up his pace. You pass through an outdoor market, nearly knocking down a Wookiee fruit cart in your haste. "Sorry!" you say to the merchant without slowing down. You are fast, but Jaylen is faster. If Jaylen doesn't stop pretty soon, you won't be able to keep up.

Jaylen leads you down a ramp toward the forest floor. You leave the safety of the Wookiee village and enter the untamed wilderness of the wroshyr tree forest. Jaylen is pulling ahead. "Please, Jaylen, let's talk this over!" There is no response.

Now you've lost sight of your friend altogether. The forest is so dense, he could be ten feet away and you wouldn't be able to see him. If you keep pressing forward into the wilderness, you risk losing your way back. Maybe you should just turn back and leave Jaylen to his fate.

You hear a rustling in the nearby bushes. Cautiously you approach them to investigate. "Jaylen? Is that you?"

Suddenly, out from the brush jumps a scaly beast

the size of a tiger. The creature slams into your chest, knocking you flat on your back. Quickly, you reach for your lightsaber, but it's no use; the beast knocks it out of your grasp with its paw. As its toothy mouth opens above your head you can smell the stench of rotting meat coming up from the beast's belly. In a few seconds, barring a miracle, you'll be joining that meat as the creature's next meal!

Turn to page 143.

The moment you and Jaylen step through the doorway, every head in the cantina turns your way. Wookiee exiles, wayward merchants, and even a few bounty hunters make up most of the clientele. You and Jaylen stick out like a pair of tauntauns on the Dune Sea.

"A shapeshifter, huh?" you whisper as you scan the crowd of scowling faces looking your way. "Any one of these guys could be Goomi. Where do we start?"

From behind you, Jaylen says, "Um . . . I think he found us!"

When you turn around to face your friend, suddenly you are seeing double. There are two Jaylens looking back at you, identical in every way. You've found your shapeshifter, all right, but now you've got another problem.

"Which one of you is Jaylen?" you ask.

"I am!" the two Jaylens reply in unison.

"Don't listen to him," the Jaylen on the left insists. "The other guy is Goomi. He's just messing with us!"

"No, I'm not! *He's* Goomi!" the Jaylen on the right counters.

You're going to have to handle this logically. If you ask a question only the real Jaylen could answer, picking out your friend shouldn't be a problem. "Listen up, you two. When did we first become friends?" you ask.

The Jaylen on the left quickly answers, "That's easy, silly. We've been friends since the first day we were sent to the Jedi Temple!"

The Jaylen on the right, however, says, "It wasn't until we were paired up in our lightsaber class. Don't tell me you've forgotten?"

Of course you know the answer. The real Jaylen is . . .

If you think the real Jaylen is the one on the left, turn to page 108.

If you think the real Jaylen is the one on the right, turn to page 112.

"You're right, Jaylen. We have to find Master Eerin. Before her last transmission cut out, she was on her way down to the surface."

Upon descending toward the research facility on Akoshissss, you discover that the lifeless moon isn't as empty as you were led to believe. The facility itself is protected by an energy shield. You'll never get past that with just your ship's blasters. Even more troubling are hundreds of droids circling the base. This is a mission for a clone army, not a Padawan!

Suddenly you hear a piercing explosion and your starfighter begins to shake. "Please tell me you just hit some turbulence," Jaylen says.

"Not unless your idea of turbulence carries laser cannons," you reply. "I've got tri-fighters on my tail!"

None of your evasive actions can shake the tri-fighters. Suddenly, things look a lot worse. "There's a large ship approaching, and it's coming in fast!"

You are engulfed in shadow as the large ship looms over your tiny starfighter. You brace for the worst . . .

Turn to page 59.

The creature is about to bitc, when all of a sudden you hear a familiar voice yell out, "Noooo!" Jaylen does a flying kick, hitting the beast in the head and sending it rolling away from you. You knew your friend would never abandon you!

This gives you enough time to summon your lightsaber to your hand. Your weapon sparks to life, illuminating the shadowy forest glade with its glowing green blade.

Jaylen ignites his own lightsaber and takes his place by your side. "Just because I saved you doesn't mean I'll go back with you. I'm through with the Jedi Order."

"Fair enough," you say. "We can talk things over once we've taken care of Mr. Toothy here."

Together you advance on the snarling beast. Even though it's outmatched, the creature shows no signs of backing down.

From behind you, a gruff and unfamiliar voice calls out, "Would you kindly put down those weapons and step away from my cargo?"

You turn around to see who the speaker is and find yourself face-to-face with a grizzled human mercenary with a blaster pointed right at you.

"The name's Crovan Dane, the greatest hunter in the galaxy, and that creature over there is my prey."

What a twist of luck! Chance has brought you to your original target. Perhaps the Force is still with you after all!

Turn to page 147.

"I'm sorry, but we're not interested," you tell the
Toydarian. He flies off in a huff. "Jaylen, we have
to do something about that Neimoidian. The Trade
Federation has no jurisdiction here, and that Wookiee
clearly doesn't want to go with him."

"All right! Let's fire up our lightsabers and show
those MagnaGuards how a real Jedi fights," Jaylen
says.

"Wait! I've got a plan," you say. "We save our
lightsabers for a *last resort*. Follow my lead."

You pull back your hood, letting your Padawan
braid show. Side by side, you and Jaylen approach the
Separatist calmly and confidently, like Jedi. The nearby
merchants and travelers, sensing trouble, clear away
from the Neimoidian's ship. Any element of surprise
you had is now gone.

"What have we here?" the Neimoidian sneers.

"Kashyyyk is protected by the Republic," you say
as sternly as you can. "Release the Wookiee or face
arrest by Jedi."

"Ha ha ha! What is this? Two Jedi whelps dare
threaten me, the great Gama Bankor? You could
get hurt if you aren't careful." As if on cue, his
MagnaGuards step forward menacingly. "Walk away,

children, and I will forget this offense."

Jaylen's face is turning red from the insult. "Who are you calling children?!" If you don't do something to stop him, this will surely end in a fight—and one you aren't likely to win.

"Wait!" you shout.

Turn to page 79.

Crovan Dane is not alone. He is joined by a mighty Wookiee warrior who has a patch over one eye and a dangerous-looking bowcaster in his hands. "Tranquilize the katarn and get it back to its cage, buddy," Crovan says to his partner. "I'll take care of these two."

The Wookiee roars in the affirmative.

Crovan looks you and Jaylen over and says, "You know the Republic must be in trouble if they're sending Padawan to do a Jedi's work."

"We may be young, but we are still trained in the ways of the Jedi," you say with confidence. "You would be wise to surrender to us."

"It sounds like you bought the whole 'Jedi Code' nonsense hook, line, and sinker," Crovan says. "But your friend there—Jaylen, was it? He seems to be smarter than that. I couldn't help but overhear that you're ready to call it quits."

Jaylen looks curiously at Crovan. "Why do you care?"

Crovan smiles. "Because I used to be a Jedi initiate myself, but I dropped out before becoming a Padawan. I couldn't take the rules and all those pompous old men on the Council acting like they know what's best for the galaxy. As soon as I was old enough to pilot my own ship, I hightailed it from Coruscant and became a mercenary. If you're looking to make an exit, kid, I'd be more than willing to help show you the ropes. Someone with your training would have no trouble making good money as a bounty hunter or bodyguard."

"Don't listen to him," you urge, but you have a feeling Jaylen's already made up his mind.

"I'm sorry," Jaylen says. "He's right. The Jedi Order is no place for me. If you're really my friend, you'll turn around and let me do what's right for me. Go back to the Wookiee village and take care of Grakchawwaa's problem."

If you agree to let Jaylen go with Crovan, turn to page 31.

If you refuse to let Jaylen go with Crovan, turn to page 152.

By the time you return to Master Eerin on Akoshissss, the battle is over. The droid forces have been quashed and the renegade scientist Bitt Panith is under arrest. With the mission a success, it's time to return home.

Back at the Jedi Temple, you run into your friend Ahsoka Tano, who has just returned from Tatooine with Generals Kenobi and Skywalker.

"You'll never believe what happened on my mission," she says. "I fought the assassin Asajj Ventress all by myself! And there was this baby Hutt. He was pretty cute, in a gross sort of way."

What an adventure! So how was your first mission? I hear the battle was pretty exciting."

"Well . . . I didn't actually see the battle," you say. After hearing about Ahsoka's adventures, your trip to Trandosha pales in comparison.

From behind you, a voice says, "So this is Bant Eerin's new Padawan. My old friend told me how proud she is of your skills as a negotiator." You turn around to see who is speaking and discover none other than Obi-Wan Kenobi!

"M-master Kenobi!" you stammer. "It was nothing, really. I just talked . . ."

Obi-Wan pats you on the shoulder and smiles. "Just talking is one of the hardest skills a Jedi can master. Using a lightsaber, that's easy! Let me tell you a story about one of my first missions with my former Master, Qui-Gon Jinn. We were on our way to the Rutan system to negotiate a peace between the Rutanians and the Senalis . . ."

As you listen to Master Kenobi's story, you realize that being an ambassador isn't such a bad thing after all!

THE END

Yoda is waiting for you when you step through the archway into the lush Jedi Meditation Gardens. "Come closer, initiates. Speak with you, I would."

As you and Jaylen approach the diminutive Jedi Master, you feel his ancient eyes staring at you. It's almost as if he's trying to peer into your heart.

"Without a Padawan, Master Bant Eerin remains, but an excellent mentor would she will be," Yoda says. "One of you, her Padawan I will make."

You and Jaylen look at each other nervously. So Yoda does plan on promoting, but only one of you?

Yoda closes his eyes tightly, but somehow you feel his gaze more strongly than ever. "Very close your two hearts are. Hard to choose it is." He opens his eyes and sighs. "Hmm . . . A final test you must take. See if your mind is at one with the Force, we will. Concentrate . . . Concentrate . . ."

Think of a number between one and ten. Now double it. Then add twenty. Next, divide by two. Finally, subtract the number you first thought of. What is left? Turn to that page to see if your mind is at one with the Force.

You shake your head. "No way, Jaylen," you say. "It's because I am your friend that I can't let you throw your life away by joining this criminal."

Your words seem to have cut to Jaylen's core. He hangs his head in shame, unable to look you in the eye.

Crovan Dane is also shaken by your decision. He points his blaster at you and growls. "Wrong answer, kid."

Just as the mercenary is about to pull the trigger, Jaylen ignites his lightsaber and swings it at Crovan's gun, slicing the barrel in half.

"No," Jaylen says. "It was exactly the right answer." He turns to you and looks you square in the eyes. "I'm sorry. I've been such a fool. Maybe I have ruined my chances of being a Jedi, but I could never turn on my best friend."

You give Jaylen a comforting smile. "Hey, we all make mistakes." You reignite your own lightsaber and add, "What do you say we arrest this scoundrel and his partner and take them back to Coruscant together?"

Jaylen nods. "Let's do it!"

With his blaster destroyed, Crovan puts up little resistance before surrendering. His partner, the Wookiee Tahnchukka, soon follows Crovan's lead.

You follow the two back to their camp and find dozens of cages full of dangerous beasts like the katarn you battled earlier. Apparently they were planning to sell these beasts to Doctor Bitt Panith on Akoshissss for some kind of experimental project. It's a good thing you found him when you did.

With your prisoners in tow, you return to the Wookiee village.

Turn to page 28.

You are awoken by a loud rumbling. You are in a starship in the middle of planetary reentry. Your wrists are bound behind your back. To your right you see Jaylen, similarly bound. Piloting the ship is your betrayer, Goomi.

"Ah, you're awake! Just in time for our arrival on Coruscant," Goomi says. "Master Ziro will know what to do with you. He always does."

Goomi pilots the ship to the backstreets of one of Coruscant's seedier neighborhoods. This must be the lair of crime lord Ziro the Hutt.

Once the ship lands, a pair of MagnaGuards come out to greet you. "Master Ziro wants to see you at once, Goomi," the robotic bodyguard says.

The MagnaGuards escort the three of you to Ziro the Hutt's office. The giant sluglike crime lord paces back and forth across the room. He doesn't look pleased to see you.

Turn to page 45.

Cautiously you pilot your ship toward the freighter. You've got a bad feeling about this . . .

Suddenly one of the seemingly disabled starfighters powers up and flies straight for you! If your memory serves you, the ship is a Sabaoth starfighter, dangerous enough on its own, but this one looks like it's had a few modifications. Four laser cannons, a pair of heavy blasters, a tractor beam, and a bank of torpedoes that are locked on to your ship and ready to be fired.

"Bounty hunter!" Jaylen shouts.

You know he's probably right. After all, you're in Trandoshan space, and the lizard-like species take to bounty hunting like a Gungan takes to water. You're outgunned. Your only chance to escape is to outmaneuver the bounty hunter.

"Let me fly! You know I'm the better pilot," Jaylen urges. "I can get us out of here."

If you try to outmaneuver the bounty bunter yourself, turn to page 85.

If you pass the controls over to Jaylen, turn to page 74.

As much as you hate to see your friend throw away his life like this, you are determined not to let his decisions jeopardize the mission. "Good-bye, Jaylen," you whisper as he disappears into the crowds. Maybe he'll come back, you hope to yourself, but something inside you tells you that isn't likely.

While you wait for the clone troopers to arrive, Chewbacca tells you everything he knows about Quaagan, the Wookiee traitor. Apparently, he has left his village and is hiding in a remote outpost, built into the side of a sheer cliff, where his Separatist contacts can send him aid without being seen by Grakchawwaa's loyal forces.

"What can you tell me about the Separatists?" you ask.

Chewbacca shakes his shaggy head. He has not seen them himself, but he hears that whoever Quaagan is dealing with reports to Count Dooku directly. If that's true, you face a dangerous foe indeed.

A few hours later, the reinforcements Master Eerin promised you have arrived. It's a Republic gunship, the workhorse of the Republic's military. This one is emblazoned with a jungle rancor across the side. As the ship approaches the Wookiee spaceport, you get a closer look at the crew: a dozen of the Republic's finest clone troopers, their white armor shimmering in the afternoon sun. So much firepower, and it's all under your command!

You and your Wookiee guide board the gunship and, after brief introductions, debrief them on the mission. "Chewbacca here will guide us to Quaagan's hold," you say. "We will approach on foot to avoid detection. Tell the men to be ready for climbing."

For the next few minutes at least you can just sit back, relax, and enjoy the view of Kashyyyk's lush forests. At least, you try to relax, but you can't get Jaylen out of your mind. Where could he have gone?

Turn to page 7.

"There is something, Master Eerin," you confess. "Jaylen Kos, a fellow student from the Jedi Temple, came along for the mission . . . without Master Yoda's permission."

"You brought a *youngling* with you?" Bant Eerin asks. Even though your Jedi Master is present only as a hologram, you can feel her disapproving look burning into you.

"I didn't exactly *bring* him," you say. "He kinda sorta snuck onboard my ship." An angry Jaylen kicks your foot.

"Thank you for telling me this, Padawan," Eerin says. "The battlefield is no place for an unsupervised youngling. Jaylen Kos must take your ship and return to Coruscant at once. You can return with the clone troopers when the mission is over. May the Force be with you." Bant Eerin's hologram flickers and cuts out.

You turn to your friend, afraid to make eye contact. "I'm sorry, Jaylen," you say. "She would have found out eventually." And in your heart, you know it was the right thing to do.

Jaylen glares at you, clearly feeling betrayed. "Thanks a lot, *friend*," Jaylen says accusingly. "Master Yoda already hates me. Can you imagine the trouble

I'll be in when he finds out? I'll never be a Jedi!"

You quickly try to console him. "Jaylen, I'm sure it's not as bad as you think. Master Yoda and the others are very understanding."

"Maybe to a teacher's pet like you," Jaylen scoffs. "Forget it. I don't want to be a stupid Jedi anyway. If the Jedi aren't prepared to train me, then I'll find someone who is!"

And with that Jaylen runs off into the crowds, leaving you alone with a confused Chewbacca.

If you take off in pursuit of Jaylen, turn to page 138.
If you let your friend go and continue with your mission, turn to page 156.

"Criminals or not, we're in this together," you say to Jaylen. "We'll worry about what to do about Goomi after Crovan's surrendered."

You ignite your lightsaber and step into the camp. "Give it up, Crovan. You're outnumbered."

Crovan and Tahnchukka raise their hands and surrender. That was easy!

"All right, Goomi. You can tell your Master that Crovan will be taken care of by the Jedi Council."

The shapeshifter scratches his scaly chin; he must be scheming again. "Not so fast, Jedi. Master Ziro needs his money. We'll deliver this cargo to Akoshissss and collect the payment first."

"But we came here to keep Crovan from making that delivery!"

Goomi spins around, a stun blaster now in his hand. "I'm making the rules now, Jedi!" He squeezes the trigger.

Turn to page 154.